Have you got them all?

A Note from Enid Blyton's Daughter

Dear Readers,

Enid Blyton wrote *The Naughtiest Girl In The School* when I
was eight years old and it has always been one of my favourites.
It appeared as a serial in Enid Blyton's little magazine called
Sunny Stories, which came out every Friday. My friends and I
would have to wait a whole week before the next chapter came
out. It was the first school story that Enid Blyton had written
and I longed for the proper book to be published.

Enid Blyton was not only a writer for children, she was also
involved in the editing and writing of books for teachers. She
was a trained Froebel and Montessori teacher and had run her
own school before she married.

She was very interested in the world of education and especially
a mixed boarding school called Summerfields, which was opened
by A. S. Neill in 1923. He believed that the school should be
governed by the children themselves with the teachers only taking
part if asked to by the children.

In the *Naughtiest Girl* series, Whyteleafe School is run in the
same way with a meeting held every week in the school hall.
The head boy and girl presided over the meeting aided by twelve
monitors chosen by the other children. It was a kind of school

Parliament, where the children made their own rules, heard grumbles and complaints, judged one another and punished bad behaviour. All problems were discussed and decided by the children and only in very difficult situations were the head teachers asked for their advice.

Of all the school series this is my favourite. The way the school is run has always made me more interested in the characters, and I think, adds to the excitement of the story. I hope you enjoy reading them.

With love from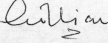

The Naughtiest Girl again

Enid Blyton

Hodder
Children's
Books

A division of Hachette Children's Books

First published in Great Britain in 1942 by George Newnes
This edition published in 2007 by Hodder Children's Books

For further information on Enid Blyton,
please contact www.blyton.com

16

A Catalogue record for this book is available
from the British Library

ISBN: 978 0 340 91770 1

Typeset in Sabon by Avon DataSet Ltd, Bidford-on-Avon, Warks

Printed and bound by CPI Group (UK) Ltd, Croydon, CR0 4YY

Hodder Children's Books
a division of Hachette Children's Books
338 Euston Road, London NW1 3BH
An Hachette UK company
www.hachette.co.uk

Contents

1 Back at Whyteleafe

Elizabeth was excited. The long summer holidays were almost over, and it was time to think of going back to school. Her mother, Mrs Allen, was busy getting all her things ready, and Elizabeth was helping her to pack the big trunk.

'Oh, Mummy, it's fun to think I'll see all my friends again soon!' said Elizabeth. 'It's lovely to be going back to Whyteleafe School once more. The winter term ought to be great fun.'

Her mother looked at Elizabeth and laughed.

'Elizabeth,' she said, 'do you remember what a fuss you made about going away to school for the first time last term? Do you remember how you said you would be so naughty and disobedient that you would soon be sent back home again? I'm glad to see you so happy this term – looking forward to going back.'

'Yes, I was stupid and silly,' said Elizabeth, going red as she remembered herself a few months back. 'Goodness, when I remember the things I said and did! Do you know, I wouldn't even share the cakes and things I took back? And I was so awfully rude and naughty in class – and I just wouldn't go to bed at the right time or do anything I was told. I was quite, quite determined to be sent back home!'

'And after all you weren't sent back, because you found you wanted to stay,' said Mrs Allen, with a smile. 'Well, well – I hope you won't be the naughtiest girl in the school *this* term.'

'I don't expect I shall,' said Elizabeth. 'I shan't be the best either – because I do fly into tempers, you know, and I don't think before I speak. I'm sure to get into trouble of some sort! But never mind, I'll get out of it again, and I'll really do my best this term.'

'Good girl,' said her mother, shutting down the lid of the trunk. 'Now look, Elizabeth – this is your tuck-box. I've put a tin of toffees in, a big chocolate cake, a tin of shortbread, and a large pot of blackcurrant jam. That's all I can get in. But I think it's enough, don't you?'

'Oh, yes, thank you, Mummy,' said Elizabeth joyfully. 'The others will love all those. I wonder if Joan's mother will give her a tuck-box this term.'

Joan was Elizabeth's friend. She had been to stay with Elizabeth in the summer holidays and the two had had a lovely time together. Then Joan had gone back home again for a week or two before school began. Elizabeth was looking forward to seeing her friend again – what fun to sleep in the same dormitory together, to sit in the same form, and play the same games!

Elizabeth had told her mother all about Whyteleafe School. It was a school for boys and girls together, and the children ruled themselves, and were seldom punished by the masters or mistresses. Every week a big school Meeting was held, and all the children had to attend. The head boy and girl were the Judges, and twelve monitors, chosen by the children themselves, were the Jury. Any grumbles or complaints had to be brought to the Meeting, and if any child had behaved wrongly, the children themselves thought out a suitable punishment.

Poor Elizabeth had suffered badly at the weekly meetings, for she had been so naughty and disobedient, and had broken every rule in the school. But now she had come to see that good behaviour was best not only for herself but for the whole school too, and she was very much looking forward to everything. Perhaps this term she could show just how good she could be, instead of just how naughty!

She was to leave the next day. Everything was packed up. She had a new lacrosse stick and a new hockey stick, for both games were played at Whyteleafe. Elizabeth was very proud of these. She had never played either game before, but she meant to be very good indeed at them. How she would run! What a lot of goals she would shoot!

Her mother took her up to London to catch the train that was ready to take her and the other girls and boys to the school. Elizabeth danced on to the London platform, and cried out in delight to see all her friends waiting there.

'Joan! You're here first! Oh, how do you do, Mrs Townsend? Have you come to see Joan off?'

'Yes,' said Mrs Townsend. 'How do you do, Mrs Allen? I'm glad to see the naughtiest girl in the school looking so delighted to be going back to Whyteleafe again!'

'Oh, don't tease me,' said Elizabeth. 'I'm not the naughtiest girl any more! Oh, look – there's Nora! Nora, Nora! Did you have good holidays?'

Nora, tall and dark, turned and waved to Elizabeth. 'Hallo, kid!' she said. 'So you're coming back again, are you? Dear, dear, we shall have to make a whole set of new rules for you, I expect.'

Mrs Townsend laughed. 'There you are, Elizabeth!' she said. 'Everybody will tease you. They will find it hard to forget how naughty you were in your first term at Whyteleafe!'

'Look! There's Harry!' cried Joan. 'Harry! You know those rabbits you gave Elizabeth and me last term? Well, they're grown up now, and they've got babies of their own. I've got two of them with me to take back to school for my own pets.'

'Good!' said Harry. 'Hallo, Elizabeth! How brown you are! Hi, John – here's Elizabeth! You'd better start planning your winter gardening with her.'

John Terry came up. He was a tall, strong boy, about twelve years old, so fond of gardening that he was head of the school garden, under Mr Johns, a master. He and Elizabeth had planned all kinds of things for the winter term.

'Hallo, Elizabeth!' he said. 'Have you brought that gardening book you promised? Good! We'll have some fun this term, digging, and burning up rubbish!'

The two of them talked eagerly for a minute or two, and then another boy came up, dark-haired and serious-faced. He took Elizabeth's arm.

'Hallo, Richard!' said Elizabeth. 'You are a mean thing – you said you'd write to me and you didn't! I bet you haven't practised once during the holidays!'

Richard smiled. He was a splendid musician for his age and could play both piano and violin beautifully. He and Elizabeth shared a great love for music, and the two of them had been twice encored when they played duets at the school concert.

'I went to stay with my grandfather,' he said. 'He has a really marvellous violin, and he let me use it. I just didn't think of anything but music all the time I was on holiday. Thanks for your card. The writing was so bad I could only read your name at the end – but still, thanks all the same!'

'Oh!' began Elizabeth indignantly, and then she saw the twinkle in Richard's eye, and laughed. 'Oh, Richard, I hope Mr Lewis lets us learn duets again this term!'

'Say goodbye to your people now,' said Miss Ranger, coming up to the little group. 'The train is just going. Find places as quickly as you can.'

Miss Ranger was Elizabeth's form-mistress. She was strict, very just, and quite a jolly person. Elizabeth and Joan were delighted to see her again. She smiled at them and went on to the next group.

'Do you remember how Miss Ranger sent you out of the room last term for flipping your rubber at people?' said Joan, with a giggle, as the two of them jumped into a carriage. Elizabeth laughed. She turned to her mother.

'Goodbye, Mummy darling!' she said. 'You needn't worry about me *this* term! I'll do my best, not my worst!'

The engine whistled loudly. Every boy and girl was now safely on the train. The mothers, fathers, uncles, and aunts waved goodbye. The train pulled out of the station and London was soon left behind.

'Now we're really off!' said Elizabeth. She looked round the carriage. Belinda was there, and Nora. Harry had got in, and John Terry too. John was already pulling out a bag of sweets. He offered them round. Everybody took one, and soon chatter and laughter filled the carriage, as the children told about their holidays.

'Is there anybody new this term, I wonder?'

said Joan. 'I haven't seen anyone yet.'

'Yes – there are two or three newcomers,' said John. 'I saw a boy down the other end of the train, and a couple of girls. I should think they'd be in your form. I didn't like the look of the boy much – sulky-looking creature!'

'What are the girls like?' asked Joan. But John hadn't noticed. 'Anyway, we shall soon see what they're like when we arrive,' said Joan. 'I say, Elizabeth, what have you got in your tuck-box? My mother has given me a huge box of chocolates, a ginger cake, a tin of golden syrup, and a jam sponge sandwich.'

'Sounds good!' said Elizabeth. The children began to talk about their tuck-boxes, and the time flew past as the train roared on its way.

At last the long journey was over and the train came to a stop at a little country platform. The boys and girls jumped down from their carriages and ran to take their places in two coaches.

'Let's look out for the first glimpse of Whyteleafe School!' said Elizabeth, as the coaches rumbled off. 'Oh, look – there it is! Isn't it lovely!'

The children stared up the hill on the top of which was their school. All of them were glad to see it again. Here and there the creeper up the walls was beginning to turn red, and the windows shone in the autumn sun.

Through an enormous archway rumbled the coaches, and up to the front door. Elizabeth remembered the first time she had arrived there, five months before, at the beginning of the summer term. How she had hated it! Now she was glad to jump down the coach steps with the other children and race into the school.

She looked round for the new girls and boy. She saw them standing rather forlornly together, wondering where to go. Elizabeth took Joan's arm. 'Let's go and look after the new ones,' she said. 'They're looking a bit lost.'

'Right!' said Joan, and they went up to the three children. They were all about eleven or twelve years old, though the boy was big for his age.

'Come with us and we'll show you where to wash, and where to go for dinner,' said Elizabeth. They all looked at her gratefully. Rita, the head girl, came by just then, and beamed at Elizabeth.

'So you've taken the newcomers under your wing,' she said. 'I was just coming to see about them. Good! Thanks, Elizabeth and Joan!'

'That's the head girl,' said Elizabeth to the boy

and two girls. 'And look – that's William, our head boy. They're both fine. Come on. I'll show you the cloakrooms and we can all wash.'

Off they all went, and were soon washing and drying themselves in the big cloakroom downstairs. Then into the dining-hall they went, hungry as hunters. How glad they were to smell a good stew, and see the carrots and onions floating in it!

'It's grand to be back again!' said Elizabeth, looking happily round, and smiling at all the faces she knew. 'I wonder what adventures we'll have this term.'

'Perhaps we shan't have any,' said Joan. But she was wrong. Plenty of things were going to happen that term!

2 Settling down

Everyone soon settled down. Except for a few new children, the girls and boys were the same as the term before. Some had gone up into a higher form, and felt rather grand for the first few days. The new boy and two new girls were all in Elizabeth's form.

Miss Ranger took down their names: 'Jennifer Harris, Kathleen Peters, Robert Jones.'

Jennifer was a jolly-looking girl, with straight hair cut short, and a thick fringe. Her brown eyes twinkled, and the other girls felt that she would be good fun.

Kathleen Peters was a pasty-faced girl, very plain and spotty. Her hair was greasy-looking, and she had a very unpleasant expression, almost a scowl. Nobody liked her at all, those first few days.

Robert Jones was a big boy for his age, with a rather sullen face, though when he smiled he was quite different.

'I don't like Robert's mouth, do you?' said Joan to Elizabeth. 'His lips are so thin and pursed up. He doesn't look very kind.'

'Oh well, we can't help our mouths!' said Elizabeth.

'I think you're wrong there,' said Joan. 'I think people make their own faces, as they grow.'

Elizabeth laughed. 'Well, it's a pity poor Kathleen Peters didn't make a better face for herself,' she said.

'Sh!' said Joan. 'She'll hear!'

The first week went by slowly. New books were given out, and lovely new pencils and pens. The children were given their places in class, and Joan and Elizabeth sat next to one another, much to their delight. They were by the window and could see out into the flowery garden.

Any child who wanted to could help in the garden. John Terry was willing to give anyone a patch, providing they would promise to keep it properly. These little patches, backing on to an old sunny wall, were interesting little spots. Some children liked to grow salads, some grew flowers, and one child, who loved roses better than anything, had six beautiful rose-trees and nothing else.

Elizabeth didn't want a patch. She wanted to help John in the much bigger garden of which he was in charge. She was longing to make plans with him about it. She had all kinds of ideas about gardens, and had read her gardening book from end to end twice during the holidays.

The children were allowed to have their own pets, though not dogs or cats, as these were too difficult to deal with, and could not be kept in cages. Some children had rabbits, some had guinea-pigs, a few had fantail pigeons that lived in a big pigeon-house on a pole, and one or two had canaries or goldfish. It was fun having pets. Not all the children kept them – only those who were fond of animals or birds. The pets were kept in a big airy shed not far from the stables where the horses were kept that the children were allowed to ride.

Hens and ducks were kept, of course, and although these belonged to the school, any child who wished could help to care for them and feed them. There were three beautiful Jersey cows in the meadow, too, and one girl and boy milked these every day. They had to be up early in the morning, but they didn't mind at all. It was fun!

Jennifer Harris had some pets. They were small

white mice, and she was very fond of them indeed. They were kept in a big cage, and she cleaned it out every day, so that it was spotless. No one else had white mice at that time, and Elizabeth and Joan went with Jennifer to see them.

'Aren't they sweet?' said Jennifer, letting a mouse run up her sleeve. 'Do you see their pink eyes? Elizabeth, would you like to let that one run up your sleeve? It's such a lovely feeling.'

'Well, I don't think I will, thank you,' said Elizabeth politely. 'It may be a lovely feeling to you, but it might not be for me.'

'Hallo! Are these your white mice, Jennifer?' asked Harry, coming up. 'I say, aren't they lovely? Golly, you've got one peeping out from your neck – did you know?'

'Oh yes,' said Jennifer. 'Take it, Harry. It will run up your sleeve and come out at your neck, too.'

Sure enough it did! It ran up the boy's sleeve, and soon its tiny nose was peeping out behind his collar. Joan shivered.

'I really don't think I could bear that,' she said.

The bell rang and the mice were hurriedly put back into their cage. Joan went to have a last peep at her two rabbits. They were fat and contented. She shared them with Elizabeth and was very fond of them indeed.

Teatime and supper-time the first week were lovely, because the children were allowed to take what they liked from their tuck-boxes. How they enjoyed the cakes, sandwiches, sweets, chocolates, potted meat, and jams they brought back with them! Everybody shared, though the new boy, Robert, didn't look too pleased about it, and Elizabeth noticed that Kathleen Peters did not offer any of her sweets round, though she shared her potted meat readily enough.

Elizabeth remembered how selfish she had been about sharing her own things at the beginning of her first term, so she held her tongue and said nothing.

'I can't very well blame other people for a thing I've done myself,' she thought. 'I'm jolly glad I'm different now!'

The big happening of each week was the school Meeting. The whole school attended, and any of the masters and mistresses who wished to. The two headmistresses, Miss Belle and Miss Best, always came, and Mr Johns usually came too. But they sat at the back, and did not take any part in the Meeting unless the children called upon them for help.

It was a kind of school Parliament, where the children made their own rules, heard grumbles and complaints, judged one another, and punished bad behaviour.

It was not pleasant to have one's faults brought before the whole school and discussed, but on the other hand it was much better for everyone to know their own failings and have them brought out into the open, instead of fearing them and keeping them secret, so that they grew bigger. Many a child had been cured for always of such things as cheating or lying by having the sympathy and help of the whole school.

The first school Meeting was held about a week after school began. The girls and boys filed into the gym, where a big table had been placed for the twelve monitors, who were the Jury. These had been chosen at the last Meeting of the summer term, and would remain monitors for a month, when they could either be chosen again, or others put into their place.

Everyone had to stand when William and Rita, the head boy and head girl, came into the gym. They sat down and everyone else sat too.

William knocked on the table with a small

wooden hammer, and the children were quiet.

'There isn't much to say today,' said the head boy. 'I expect the new children have been told why we hold this big Meeting every week, and what we do at it. You see at this table our twelve monitors, and you all know why they are chosen. We chose them ourselves because we can trust them to be sensible, loyal and kind, and therefore you must obey them and keep the rules they make.'

Then Rita spoke. 'I hope you have all brought your money with you. As the new children probably know, any money we have is put into this big box, and out of it we take two pounds for every person each week. Out of that you must buy anything you need, such as stamps, sweets, ribbons, shoelaces, and so on. If you want any more than two pounds you must say why, and it will be given to you if it is deserved. Now will you please get your money ready. Nora, take round the box.'

Nora got up. She took the big box and handed it down each row. The children all put in their money. The new boy, Robert Jones, looked most annoyed.

'I say,' he said, 'you know I've got a whole ten

pounds from my grandfather. I don't see why I should put it into the box. I shan't see it again!'

'Robert, some of us have too much money and some of us have too little,' explained William. 'It sometimes happens that we have a birthday and get lots of money, and sometimes we haven't any at all. Well, by putting all our money into the big box each week, we can always have two pounds to spend – the same for everyone, you see, which is quite fair – and if we need anything beyond that, we can always get it if the Jury give permission. So put in your money.'

Robert put his ten pound note in, and did not look at all pleased. His face looked even more sulky than usual!

'Cheer up!' whispered Elizabeth, but he gave her such a scowl that she said no more. Nora took the box back to the table. It was very heavy now.

Two pounds were given out to everyone, and the money went into pockets and purses. Rita and William had the same as everyone else.

'Any extra money wanted this week?' asked William, looking round the school.

Kenneth stood up. 'Could I have an extra fifty pence?' he asked. 'I borrowed a book out of the school library and I can't find it, and I've been fined fifty pence.'

'Take it out of your two pounds,' said William, and the Jury nodded in agreement. 'I don't see why the school's money should pay you for being careless, Kenneth! There are too many books lost. Pay the school library fifty pence, and you can have it back when you find the book. No extra money granted!'

A girl stood up. 'My mother is abroad and I have to write to her each week, of course, but the letters have to have a forty pence stamp on. Could I possibly have a little extra money allowed for that?'

The Jury discussed the matter. They agreed that it was hard luck on Mary to have to spend so much money on one letter each week.

'Well, you can have twenty pence extra each week,' said Rita, at last. 'That means you pay the usual amount for a stamp, and the school money pays the rest. That's quite fair.'

'Oh yes,' said Mary gratefully. 'Thank you.' Twenty pence was given to her, and she put it into her purse.

'I think that's all the business for this week,' said Rita, looking at her notes. 'You all understand that any bad behaviour, such as unkindness, disobedience, cheating, bullying, and so on, must be brought before this Meeting each week. But I hope that the new children will understand that this does not mean telling tales. Perhaps their monitor will explain everything to them.'

'Yes, I will,' said Nora.

'Now – any complaints or grumbles before we go?' asked William, looking up. But there were none. So the Meeting broke up, and the children filed out of the gym. Elizabeth was rather silent as she went. She was remembering the bad time she had had last term at the Meeting. How defiant and rude she had been! She could hardly believe it now.

She went off with Joan to feed the rabbits. One was so tame that it would lie quite peacefully in Elizabeth's arms, and she loved that.

'Isn't everything peaceful this term?' said Joan. 'I hope it goes on like this, don't you?'

But it wasn't going to be peaceful for long!

3 Elizabeth makes an enemy

It was two of the new children who disturbed the peace of the form. When Robert had settled down and found his feet, the other boys and girls found that he was spiteful and unkind. And they discovered, too, that Kathleen Peters, the white-faced, spotty girl, was so quarrelsome that it was really very difficult to be nice to her.

On the other hand, Jennifer Harris was great fun. She was a wonderful mimic and could imitate the masters and mistresses marvellously, especially Mam'zelle. Mam'zelle wagged her hands rather a lot, and her voice went up and down when she spoke. Jennifer could put on a face exactly like Mam'zelle's, and talked and wagged her hands in a manner so like her that she sent the class into fits of laughter.

'Jenny's fine,' said Elizabeth. 'But I simply can't bear Robert or Kathleen. You know, I think Robert's cruel, Joan.'

'Why do you think that?' asked Joan. 'Has he been unkind to you?'

'No – not to me,' said Elizabeth. 'But I heard someone squealing yesterday and I saw little Janet running away from him, crying. I called out to know what was wrong, but she wouldn't tell me. I believe Robert had been pinching her or something.'

'I shouldn't be surprised,' said Joan.

Belinda Green heard what they were saying and came up.

'I think Robert's a bully,' she said. 'He's always running after the smaller ones, and jumping out at them, and giving them sly pinches.'

'The hateful thing!' cried Elizabeth, who always hated any unfairness. 'Wait till I catch him! I'll jolly well report him at the very next Meeting!'

'Well, be sure to get your facts right,' said Belinda, 'or Robert will say you are telling tales, and then you won't be listened to.'

Robert came up at that moment and the three of them said no more. Robert bumped hard into Elizabeth as he passed and nearly sent her into the wall.

'Oh, I didn't see you!' he said, with a grin, and went on down the room. Elizabeth went red with rage. She took a step after Robert, but Joan pulled her back.

'He only did it to make you annoyed,' she said. 'Don't *be* annoyed!'

'I can't help being,' said Elizabeth furiously. 'Rude, clumsy thing!'

It was time to go into class then, and there was no time to do anything more. Robert was in Elizabeth's class, and she glared at him as she sat down. He made an extraordinary face at her – and they were enemies from that moment.

When Robert got nearly all his sums wrong, Elizabeth smiled with pleasure. 'Serves you right!' she said in a loud whisper. Unfortunately Miss Ranger heard it.

'Is there any need to gloat over bad work done by somebody else?' she said coldly – and then it was Robert's turn to grin with delight.

Each of them was pleased when the other did badly – though Elizabeth got more laughs out of Robert than he did out of her, for she was a clever girl and found lessons easy. Robert was much slower, though he was bigger and taller.

At games they did all they could to defeat each other. They were very often on opposite sides, and if Robert could give Elizabeth a whack over the hand with his lacrosse stick, or a blow on the ankle with his hockey stick, he would. Elizabeth was not an unkind girl, but she found herself lying in wait for Robert, too, and giving him a hard blow whenever she could.

Mr Warlow, the games master, soon noticed this, and he called the two of them to him.

'You are playing a game, not fighting a battle,' he told them gravely. 'Keep your likes and dislikes out of hockey and lacrosse, please, and play fairly.'

Elizabeth was ashamed, and stopped trying to hurt Robert – but Robert took an even greater delight in giving Elizabeth a bruise whenever he could, though now he was careful to do it when Mr Warlow was not watching.

'Elizabeth, you really are stupid to make an enemy of Robert,' said Nora one day. 'He is much bigger than you are. Keep out of his way. You'll lose your temper one day and put yourself in the wrong. That's what he's hoping for.'

But Elizabeth would not listen to advice of that sort. 'I'm not afraid of Robert!' she said scornfully.

'That isn't the point,' said Nora. 'He's only doing all this to annoy you, and if only you'd take no notice of him, and not try to pay him back, he'd soon get tired of it.'

'He's a hateful bully!' said Elizabeth.

'You're not to say things like that unless you have real proof,' said Nora, at once. 'And if you *have* real proof, then you must make a complaint at the Meeting. That's the place to accuse people of things. You know that quite well.'

Elizabeth made a sulky face and went off by herself. Why couldn't Nora believe her? Oh, well – Nora wasn't in her form and didn't know that hateful Robert as well as she, Elizabeth, knew him.

The next afternoon, after tea, Elizabeth went round to play with the rabbits. On the way she heard somebody calling out in a pleading voice:

'Please don't swing me so high! Please don't!'

Elizabeth peeped round at the swings. She saw a small boy on one, about nine years old. Robert was swinging him, and my goodness, wasn't he swinging him high!

'I feel sick!' cried the boy, whose name was Peter. 'I shall *be* sick! I shall fall off. Let me down, Robert, let me down! Don't swing me any more!'

But Robert took no notice of the small boy's shouting. His thin lips were pursed together, and with an unkind gleam in his eyes, he went on pushing the swing – high, high, higher!

Elizabeth was so angry that she had to blink her eyes to see clearly. She ran to Robert.

'Stop!' she cried. 'You're not to do that! You'll make Peter ill.'

'Mind your own business,' said Robert. 'He asked me to give him a swing and I'm giving him one. Go away, you interfering girl. You're always poking your nose where it isn't wanted.'

'Oh, I'm not!' cried Elizabeth. She tried to catch hold of the swing as it came down, to stop it, but Robert was too quick for her. He gave her a push and sent her spinning into a bush. Then he sent the swing even higher than ever.

'I'll go and tell somebody!' cried Elizabeth, picking herself up.

'Tell-tale, tell-tale!' chanted Robert, giving the swing another push. Elizabeth lost her temper completely and rushed at the aggravating boy. She caught hold of his hair and pulled at it so hard that she pulled a whole handful out! Then she slapped his face and gave him such a punch in his middle that he doubled himself up with a groan.

Elizabeth stopped the swing and helped the

trembling Peter off the seat. 'Go and be sick if you want to,' she said. 'And don't let Robert swing you any more.'

Peter staggered off, looking rather green. Elizabeth turned to face Robert, but just then three or four children came up, and neither child felt inclined to go on with the quarrel in public.

'I'll report you at the very next Meeting!' cried Elizabeth, still in a great temper. 'You just see! You'll be punished all right, you cruel, unkind boy!'

She went off, raging. Robert looked round at the interested children who had come up. 'What a temper that girl has got!' he said. 'Look here – she pulled my hair out!'

He picked up some of his dark hairs and showed them to the others. They looked surprised.

'You must have been doing something awful to make Elizabeth lose her temper like that,' said Kenneth.

'I was only giving someone a swing,' said Robert. 'Elizabeth interfered, as usual. I wish she'd leave me alone. No wonder she was called the naughtiest girl in the school last term!'

'We pinned a notice on her once, called her the

Bold Bad Girl!' said somebody, with a laugh, as he remembered how angry Elizabeth had been. 'Did you hit Elizabeth, Robert? If you did, you're mean. Girls are awfully annoying sometimes, but if you're a boy, you can't hit them.'

'I didn't touch her,' said Robert, though he knew quite well that if the others hadn't come up at that moment he would certainly have gone for Elizabeth and slapped her hard. 'She just went up in smoke and flew at me, the horrid girl!'

Elizabeth rushed off to tell Joan all that had happened. Joan listened gravely.

'Robert really is a horrid bully,' she said. 'He'll have to be stopped. But oh, Elizabeth, I do think it's rather a pity you lost your temper like that! You have got such a hot temper, you know!'

'Well, *any*one would have lost their temper if they had seen Robert swinging that poor wretched little Peter almost over the top of the swing-post!' said Elizabeth, still boiling with rage. 'He was quite green.'

'You don't suppose the Meeting will think it's telling tales if you report Robert, do you?' asked Joan doubtfully. 'If I were you, I'd ask Nora first.'

'I'll do no such thing!' cried Elizabeth. 'I'm the best judge of this! I saw what happened, didn't I?

All right then – I'll report Robert at the Meeting tomorrow, and then we'll just see what the Jury say. He'll get a dreadful shock – and he'll deserve it, too.'

Elizabeth was angry all day, and when the next day came she could hardly wait for the evening to come, to report Robert. Then he would see what happened to boys who did mean, unkind things!

Robert did not seem to be at all upset at the idea of Elizabeth reporting him. He made faces at her whenever he saw her, which made her very angry indeed.

'You'll get a shock at the Meeting tonight!' said Elizabeth. But there was a shock waiting for Elizabeth too!

4 What happened at the Meeting

The time for the weekly Meeting came. Elizabeth sat down on the form next to Belinda and Joan, longing for the moment to come when she could make a complaint about Robert. Robert sat not far away, his sullen face unsmiling, but there was a gleam in his eye when he turned to look at Elizabeth.

'I shouldn't be surprised if Robert doesn't make a complaint about you too, Elizabeth,' whispered Joan. 'He looks as if he's got something up his sleeve.'

'I don't care,' said Elizabeth. 'Wait till the Meeting hears what *I've* got to say!'

William and Rita came in, with the headmistresses and Mr Johns. The children stood up. The head girl and boy sat down, and the Meeting began.

Money was collected, though there was not very much that week. Kenneth had had a birthday and had five pounds to put into the box. Janet had a pound. Everyone was given their two pounds, and Mary got her twenty pence extra for her weekly stamp.

'Have you found the lost library book yet?' asked William, looking at Kenneth. 'We said you could have back your fifty pence fine if you did.'

'No, I haven't found it,' said Kenneth. 'I've hunted everywhere.'

'Anybody want any extra money?' asked Rita, jingling the box to see how much there was in it.

'I suppose I couldn't have any extra?' asked Ruth, standing up. 'I lost all my two pounds last week. It was a dreadful blow because I badly wanted some stamps.'

'How did you lose it?' asked Rita.

'There was a hole in my pocket,' said Ruth. 'It fell out through that, goodness knows where.'

'Did you know there was a hole in your pocket?' asked Rita.

Ruth hesitated. 'Well,' she said, 'I did know there was one coming, as a matter of fact. It was just a tiny little hole. I didn't know it had got big enough to lose money.'

'Who's your monitor?' asked William. 'Oh, you are, Nora. Do you think it was Ruth's fault?'

'Well,' said Nora, 'quite truthfully, Ruth isn't

awfully good at mending her clothes when she ought to. She lost a lovely pocket-knife last term, through a hole in a pocket – didn't you, Ruth?'

'Yes,' said Ruth, looking rather uncomfortable. 'Yes, I did. I know I should have mended that hole. I'm untidy and careless about things like that. I jolly well won't get a hole again, though. I think I shouldn't have asked for extra money, as it was my own fault.'

She sat down. The Jury began to talk to one another. A girl sitting on one of the forms stood up. It was Eileen, a kindly girl with a mass of fair curls.

'May I say something?' she asked. 'I think that as Ruth has owned up that it was her own fault, and as she really is very generous with her money when she has it, couldn't she have an extra two pounds, just for once?'

'We are just discussing that,' said Rita. 'This is what we are going to do. We will let you have a pound, Ruth, not two pounds, because we all believe you aren't quite so silly as to let a thing like this happen a third time, and you have been very honest about it. Come and take an extra pound.'

'Oh, thank you,' said Ruth, going to the table. 'I had to borrow some stamps from Belinda, and now I can pay her back without using this week's two pounds. I'll be more careful in future, Rita!'

'Any more money wanted?' asked William, knocking on the table with his hammer, for the children had begun to talk to one another. Everyone was quiet.

'It's my Granny's birthday this week,' said a small girl, getting up. 'I want to send her a card. Could I have extra money to buy it with, and for the stamp, too?'

'No,' said William. 'That should come out of your two pounds. Not granted. Any more requests?'

There were none. Elizabeth knew that the time for complaints or grumbles would come next, and she went red with excitement. William said a few words to Rita about something and then knocked for silence again.

'Any complaints or grumbles?' he asked. Elizabeth stood up – and so did Robert – but Robert was just half a second before her.

'You first, Robert,' said William. 'Sit down and take your turn next, Elizabeth.'

Elizabeth didn't sit down. She didn't mean to let Robert speak first.

'Oh, please, William!' she said. 'I have such

a serious complaint to make.'

'Well, it will keep,' said William. 'Sit down.'

'But William, it's about Robert,' began Elizabeth again, her voice rising.

'Elizabeth, do as you're told,' ordered Rita. 'You will have plenty of time to say all you want to.'

There was nothing for it but to sit down. Elizabeth was very angry. She glared at Robert, who didn't look at her at all, but stood patiently waiting to speak.

'Well, Robert, what have you to say?' asked William.

'I hope this isn't telling tales,' began Robert in a rather apologetic voice, 'but I really must complain about Elizabeth Allen's behaviour to me. I have always tried to be fair to her . . .'

'Oooooh!' cried Elizabeth indignantly. 'You know you haven't! You've . . .'

'Silence, Elizabeth!' ordered William sharply. 'You can say all you want to say in a minute. Don't interrupt. Go on, Robert.'

Elizabeth was boiling with rage. Joan put her hand on her friend's arm to try and calm her, but Elizabeth shook it off. Just wait till she had her turn to speak!

'I've always tried to be fair to her,' went on Robert in a very polite voice. 'But really, I can't let her pull my hair out and slap me in the face.'

There was an astonished silence. Everyone looked at Elizabeth. Robert went on, pleased at the surprise he had caused.

'I've got some of the hairs she pulled out in this envelope to show you, William, in case you don't believe me. And there are two or three children who will tell you it really happened. Of course, as she's a girl, I couldn't hit her back. I know she was supposed to be the naughtiest girl in the school last term, and . . .'

'You can leave that out, Robert. It has nothing to do with this,' said William at once. 'We have always found Elizabeth to be just and fair and kind so far, no matter how naughty she once was. Will you please tell us *why* Elizabeth did these extraordinary things?'

'She didn't want me to swing somebody,' said Robert. 'She's always interfering with me, whatever I do. She laughs if I make a mistake in class. Well, never mind about that. I was just swinging Peter, and he was squealing with excitement, and she came and pulled out my hair, slapped me and punched me.'

'Thank you,' said William. 'Sit down. Elizabeth, perhaps you would like to tell us if these complaints are true. Did you pull out Robert's hair and slap him?'

Elizabeth stood up, her cheeks as red as fire and her eyes flashing. 'Yes, I did!' she said. 'And he deserved it! I wish I'd pulled out more of his hair. I wish . . .'

'That's enough, Elizabeth,' said Rita, at once. 'If you can't control yourself enough to tell us properly what happened, there's no use in your saying anything.'

Elizabeth knew she was being silly. She tried her hardest to be sensible. 'Please, Rita, I'll tell my story properly,' she said. 'Then you'll see why I got so angry, and perhaps you'll say I was right to lose my temper with Robert. I was going to see my rabbits, when I heard somebody squealing out. It was Peter on the swing, and he was shouting to Robert not to swing him so high, because he was frightened.'

'Go on,' said William gravely.

'Well, I rushed over to stop the swing, and Robert sent me right over,' said Elizabeth, feeling her temper rise again as she told what had happened. 'I got up and flew at Robert to stop him swinging Peter again, because he was quite green and I thought he would fall off. And oh, William and Rita, that's not the only time that Robert has bullied the younger ones. He's a real bully, unkind and mean.'

There was a silence again. Everyone in the school knew quite well that a very serious thing had happened. Which of the two children was right? Bullying was hateful. Bad temper and fighting were wrong.

Joan was very upset. She knew quite well that Elizabeth had made up her mind to be good and do as well as she could this term, and now here was the hot-tempered girl flying into trouble almost at once! It was just no good trying to stop her. If Elizabeth saw something unfair she would rush at it in a temper and try to put it right that way. Joan couldn't see how this matter could be put right.

William and Rita spoke together in low voices. The Jury discussed the matter, too. Robert sat on his form, not even red in the face. He did not look at Elizabeth.

William knocked for silence. 'We would like to ask the boys and girls who saw the affair to report on it,' he said. 'Who saw it?'

Three children stood up. They said shortly that they had seen the hairs that Elizabeth had pulled out and had seen how red Robert's face was where it had been slapped.

'Did Robert hit back at all?' asked Rita.

'Not that we saw,' said Kenneth, and sat down, feeling sorry for Elizabeth.

'And now we will ask Peter to tell us what happened,' said William in a kindly tone. 'Stand up, Peter, and answer my questions.'

The small nine-year-old Peter stood up. His knees shook beneath him, and he felt dreadful to have the eyes of the whole School on him.

'Was Robert swinging you high?' asked William.

Peter looked across at Robert. Robert gave him a strange look. Peter spoke in a trembling voice. 'Yes – he was swinging me quite high.'

'Were you frightened?' asked William.

'N-n-n-no,' said Peter.

'Did you squeal for help?' asked Rita.

'No,' said Peter, with a look at Robert. 'I was just – just squealing for fun, you know.'

'Thank you,' said William. 'Sit down.'

Elizabeth leapt up. 'Robert must have made Peter promise to say all that!' she cried. 'Ask if there are any other young ones who would like to complain about Robert, Rita.'

Rita looked round where the younger children sat.

'Is there anyone who has a complaint to make about Robert?' she asked. 'If he has been unkind to you, or ill-treated you in any way, speak now.'

Elizabeth waited for half a dozen children to stand up and speak. But there was a complete silence! Nobody spoke, nobody complained. What a very strange thing! *Now* what was going to happen?

5 Elizabeth is very cross

The complaints to the school Meeting were so serious that the two Judges and the Jury took a long time to discuss them. In the meantime the rest of the children also discussed the matter among themselves. Not many of them were for Robert, for he was not liked, but on the other hand most of the boys and girls felt that Elizabeth had no right to lose her temper so fiercely.

'And after all,' whispered one child to another, 'she *was* the naughtiest girl in the school last term, you know.'

'Yes. We used to call her the Bold Bad Girl,' said another child. 'But she was quite all right after the half-term. She really did turn over a new leaf.'

'And I know quite well that she meant to do her very best this term,' said Harry. 'I've heard her say so heaps of times. She lost her temper with me last term, but she said she was sorry and has been absolutely decent to me ever since.'

So the talk went on, whilst Elizabeth and

Robert sat up straight, hating one another, each longing to hear that the other was to be punished.

Meanwhile, the Judges and Jury were finding things very difficult. Some of the Jury felt quite certain that Robert was a real bully – and yet not even Peter would complain, so maybe there was not much truth in what they thought. All the monitors on the Jury were fair-minded and just, and they knew quite well that they must never judge anyone unless they had real, clear proof of wrong-doing.

Again, all the Jury knew quite well how bad Elizabeth had been the term before, and yet how marvellously she had managed to conquer herself and turn over a new leaf. They could not believe that she would fight Robert just for nothing. It was all very difficult. They did not feel that they wanted to punish Elizabeth in case by any chance Robert *did* turn out to be a bully.

At last William knocked with his wooden mallet for silence. The whole school sat up, eager to know what had been decided. Elizabeth was still fiery red in the face, but Robert looked quite pale and cool.

'We find this matter very difficult to decide,' said William in his pleasant voice. 'It is quite clear that Elizabeth did lose her temper badly, and flew at Robert, but it isn't quite as clear that Robert was bullying Peter. After all, we must take Peter's word for that. He should know! But we know enough of Elizabeth to realize that she is a very just person, and it is quite plain that she thought Robert was doing something very unkind.'

There was a pause. The school listened hard. William thought for a moment and then went on:

'Very well. Elizabeth may have been mistaken, but she really believed that Robert was being unkind. So she lost her temper and flew at him to stop him. That is where you were wrong, Elizabeth. Hot temper makes you see things all muddled instead of clearly, so when you see something you disapprove of, you *must* try to keep your temper, so that you can judge things properly and not get them all exaggerated and twisted. You spoke as if you hated Robert just now, and that does *you* as much harm as it does Robert.'

'I do hate him!' burst out Elizabeth angrily.

'Well, to go on with this,' went on William, 'we have decided that unless we get much plainer proof that Robert is a bully, we can't very well either judge him or punish him. And as we are sure you really did think he was doing something mean, we shan't punish you either, Elizabeth, but you must say you are sorry to Robert for behaving so badly to him.'

The whole school thought this was a good decision. Nobody wanted Elizabeth badly punished, for they really did like the hot-headed girl. The school came to the conclusion that she must have been mistaken about Robert and therefore she really should apologize, and let the matter end there.

Elizabeth said nothing. She sat on the form, looking sulky. Robert looked pleased. This was grand! William and Rita spoke together for a moment or two, and then said a few more words to close the matter.

'Well, that is our decision, Elizabeth and Robert. You will apologize, Elizabeth, and you will accept the apology graciously, Robert. Elizabeth, guard your temper – and, Robert, see that no charge of bullying is ever made against you. If it should be, you would not be judged lightly.'

Then William spoke of other things for a few moments and broke up the meeting, for the time was getting late. The children were dismissed and filed out of the gym, all looking rather solemn. Bad temper and bullying! These were things not often dealt with at the Meeting.

Robert swaggered out, hands in pockets. He felt important and pleased. He had won *that* battle. Now Elizabeth had got to say she was sorry. Serve her right!

But Elizabeth had no intention of saying she was sorry. Joan looked in dismay at the angry face of her friend as she marched into the common-room.

'Elizabeth! There's Robert over there. For goodness' sake go and apologize now, and get it over,' she begged the angry girl.

'But I'm *not* sorry!' said Elizabeth in a loud voice, tossing back her dark curls. 'Not a bit! I'm glad I flew at Robert. How can I say I'm sorry if it's an untruth?'

'Well, you can apologize,' said Joan. 'That's only good manners. Just go up and say, "I apologize, Robert." You don't need to say anything more.'

'Well, I'm not going to,' said Elizabeth. 'The Judges and the Jury were wrong for once! Nobody can make me apologize.'

'Elizabeth, no matter what you feel, you should

be loyal to William and Rita,' said Joan, troubled. 'It isn't what you feel yourself that matters – it's what all the others feel to be right. You're one against a whole lot.'

'Well, I may be, but I'm the one who happens to be right,' said Elizabeth in a trembling voice. 'I know Robert is a bully.'

'Elizabeth, do what the Meeting says, and then we'll watch and see if we can't catch Robert at his horrid tricks,' begged Joan. 'Do it to please me. You'll make me so unhappy if you don't – and the whole school will think badly of you if you're afraid to apologize.'

'I'm not afraid!' said Elizabeth, with her eyes flashing angrily.

Joan smiled a little smile to herself. She turned away from Elizabeth. 'You *are* afraid,' she said. 'You're afraid of hurting your own silly pride.'

Elizabeth marched straight up to Robert. 'I apologize,' she said stiffly.

Robert gave a polite bow. 'I accept your apology!' he said. Elizabeth stalked off by herself. Joan ran after her.

'Leave me alone,' said Elizabeth crossly. She went into a music practice-room and sat down at the piano. She played a piece she knew, very loudly and fiercely. Mr Lewis, the music-master, looked into the room in surprise.

'Good gracious, Elizabeth!' he said. 'I've never heard that piece sound so angry before. Get up, and let me play you something *really* fierce – something with a thunderstorm or two in it.'

Elizabeth got up. Mr Lewis took her seat and played a stormy piece of music, with the wind and the sea, streaming clouds, roaring trees in it – and then the storm died down, the rain sprinkled softly, the wind ceased, the sun shone, and the music became calm and smooth.

And as she listened, the little girl felt soothed and softened too. She loved music so much. Mr Lewis glanced at her and saw that she looked peaceful instead of troubled. He played a little longer and then the bell went for Elizabeth's bedtime.

'There you are,' said Mr Lewis, shutting the piano. 'After the storm, the calm. Now go off to bed, sleep well, and don't worry your head too much about anything.'

'Thank you, Mr Lewis,' said Elizabeth gratefully. 'I do feel better now. I was all hot and bothered about something, but now I feel happier. Goodnight!'

6 Jenny's white mice

Elizabeth did not sleep very well that night. She tossed and turned, thinking of the Meeting, of 'that hateful Robert', as she called him to herself, of the apology she had had to make – and she made plans to catch Robert when he was being unkind to any of the younger ones.

'Yes – I'll watch and wait and catch him properly,' said Elizabeth to herself. 'He *is* a bully, I know he is – and sooner or later I'll catch him!'

Elizabeth was heavy-eyed and tired the next day. She did her lessons badly, especially French, and Mam'zelle was cross with her.

'Elizabeth! How is it that you did not learn your French verbs yesterday?' scolded Mam'zelle. 'That is not good. You sit there, half asleep, and you pay no attention at all. I am not pleased with you.'

Robert grinned to himself, and Elizabeth saw him. She bit her lip to stop herself from being rude to both Robert and Mam'zelle.

'Well, have you no tongue?' asked Mam'zelle impatiently. 'Why did you not learn your verbs, I said?'

'I *did* learn them,' said Elizabeth truthfully. 'But somehow I've forgotten them this morning.'

'Then you will please learn them sometime today and remember them!' said Mam'zelle, her dark eyes flashing. 'You will come and say them to me when you know them.'

'All right,' said Elizabeth sulkily. But Mam'zelle would not let that pass. She rapped on the desk and spoke sharply.

'You will not say "All right" to me in that rude way! You will say "Very good, Mam'zelle."'

'Very good, Mam'zelle,' said Elizabeth, knowing quite well that Robert was enjoying her scolding immensely, and wishing that she could pull some more hairs out of his dark head.

After that the lesson went on smoothly, for Elizabeth was determined not to give Robert any more chances to crow over her. But she did not do so well as usual in anything, for as soon as she had a moment to think, she began to plan how she might catch Robert being unkind to someone.

Belinda and Joan and Nora had a little talk together, whilst Elizabeth was having her music lesson that day.

'We'll have to keep Elizabeth away from Robert for a few days if we can,' said Joan. 'She just hates him, and, you know, she has such a quick temper that she's quite likely to fly at him again if he makes a rude face at her.'

'After a few days she won't feel so badly about it all,' said Nora. 'We'll try and get her to come down into the town with us, or to garden with John, or something like that – the less she sees of Robert the better. I can't say I want to see very much of him myself!'

So for the next few days Elizabeth found that she was always being rushed off somewhere.

'Come and help me to choose a new ribbon, Elizabeth!' Joan would beg. 'I really must get one.' And down to the town the two would go.

'Elizabeth, come and practise catching the ball at lacrosse with me,' Nora would say. 'You're getting quite good. A little more practice and you'll be first-rate.'

Then Elizabeth would beam with pride and go to fetch her lacrosse stick.

'Elizabeth, John wants you and me to go and

help him to pile up rubbish for a bonfire!' Belinda would call. 'Coming?'

And off Elizabeth would go again, so that she hardly saw Robert at all, except in class. But she did not forget what she had planned to do, and when she had a chance she watched to see if any of the smaller children were being bullied.

But she saw nothing of the sort. Robert went about his own business and seemed to keep right away from the younger ones. He knew quite well that Elizabeth was watching for him to do something bad again, and he wasn't going to give her the chance to catch him. She would soon get tired of that.

Robert was immensely fond of horses, and rode as often as he could. He was not allowed to look after them, because only the bigger boys and girls were allowed to do that, but he spent as much time as he could hanging round the stables, and talking to the brown-eyed horses, who put their heads out over the stable doors when they saw him. Robert took no interest in the other pets at all, much to the annoyance of the other children, who always loved to show off their pets to anyone.

So, what with Robert going out riding and the

other girls taking Elizabeth off with them as often as they could, the two enemies had few chances to meet and quarrel. It was only in class that they could show their dislike of one another.

Robert was so anxious not to give Elizabeth any chance of jeering at him that he worked extra hard, and took enormous care with his home-work. Miss Ranger, the form-mistress, was surprised and pleased to find Robert making such progress with everything, and she praised him.

'Robert, you are doing very well,' she said. 'I shouldn't be surprised if you are top of the class one week this term, if you work like this!'

Robert went red with pleasure. He was really a lazy boy, and had never been anywhere near the top of his form, even at his old school. Elizabeth was annoyed to hear Miss Ranger say this. Why, she, Elizabeth, could easily be top of the form if she wanted to! She would work like anything and just show Robert he couldn't get to the top whilst she was in the form!

So she worked very hard too; but both children were working hard for the wrong reason – to spite one another! So they did not enjoy their work at all, which was a great pity.

Then for a time both Robert and Elizabeth

forgot their quarrel in the interest of something else. Jennifer's white mice made a great disturbance, and Jenny nearly got into serious trouble!

Her white mice had a family of nine small baby mice, most adorable creatures with soft white fur, woffly noses, pink eyes, and tiny tails. Jenny loved these very much indeed, and it was quite a sight to see the little girl with half a dozen mice running up and down her sleeves.

'Jenny, put them back, the bell's gone,' said Elizabeth one morning. 'Hurry! You'll be late, and Miss Ranger isn't in a very good temper this morning.'

'Oh, golly, I can't find them all,' said Jenny, feeling all over her body for the baby mice. 'Wherever have they gone? Is there one down my back, Elizabeth?'

'Oh, Jenny, how can you let them do that!' cried Elizabeth. 'No, there isn't one down your back. They must be all there in the cage now. Do come on. I shan't wait for you if you're a second longer.'

Jenny shut the cage-door carefully and latched it. Then she ran off with Elizabeth, and they arrived in their classroom panting, just as Miss Ranger also arrived.

They took their places. The lesson was

geography, and the class were learning about Australia and the big sheep-farms there. Jenny had a seat in the first row, just in front of Elizabeth and Joan.

And, in the middle of the lesson, Elizabeth saw the nose of a white mouse peeping out at the back of Jenny's neck! Jenny felt it too. She wriggled, put up her hand and pushed the mouse down. It disappeared.

Elizabeth so badly wanted to giggle that she did not dare to look up at all. When she *did* look up, she saw the mouse peeping out of Jenny's left sleeve. It looked round at Elizabeth with pink eyes. Then it disappeared again.

Jenny found the mouse very tickly indeed. She wriggled about. She tried to make the mouse go up to her shoulder where it could be comfortable and go to sleep. But it wasn't at all sleepy. It was a very lively mouse indeed. It ran all round Jenny, sniffing here and there at shoulder straps and tapes, and Jenny couldn't stop wriggling.

Miss Ranger noticed her. 'Jenny! What in the world is the matter with you this morning? Do sit still.'

'Yes, Miss Ranger,' said Jenny. But a second later the mouse went under her left arm-hole, where Jenny really was very ticklish indeed, and the little girl gave a giggle and another wriggle. Miss Ranger looked up.

'Jennifer! You are behaving like a child in the kindergarten! And Elizabeth, what is the matter with *you*?'

There was nothing the matter with Elizabeth except that she simply could *not* help laughing at Jenny, because she knew so well why Jenny was wriggling. The mouse popped its head out of Jenny's neck and stared at Elizabeth and Joan. The two girls tried to stop their giggles, but the more they tried to stop, the worse they got.

'This class is a disgrace this morning,' said Miss Ranger impatiently. 'Come up here to the board, Jennifer, and point out some things to me on the map. If you can't *sit* still, perhaps you can stand still!'

Jenny got up and went to the board. The mouse was pleased to find it was having a ride, and it scampered all round Jenny's back. Jenny put her hand behind her and tried to stop it.

'Jenny! What *is* wrong?' asked Miss Ranger. By this time the whole class knew about Jenny's mouse, and everyone was bending over their books, red in the face, trying their hardest not to giggle. A little squeal came from Kenneth, and Miss Ranger put down her book in despair.

'There is some joke going on,' she said. 'Well, let me share it. If it's funny, we'll all have a good laugh. If it isn't, we'll get on with the lesson. Now, what's the joke?'

Nobody told her. Jenny looked at the class with pleading eyes, begging them silently not to give her away. The mouse also looked out of Jenny's sleeve. Miss Ranger was really puzzled.

And then the mouse decided to explore the world a bit! So out it ran, jumped on to Miss Ranger's desk, and sat up to wash its whiskers.

The class went off into shouts of laughter. Miss Ranger looked down in the greatest astonishment. She had not seen where the mouse had come from.

'How did this mouse come here?' she asked.

'It jumped from my sleeve, please, Miss Ranger,' said Jenny. 'I was playing with my white mice when the bell rang, and I suppose I didn't put them all back into the cage. This one was still up my sleeve.'

'So that's the joke!' said Miss Ranger, beginning to smile. 'Well, I agree it's a good joke, and no wonder everyone laughed. But it's not a joke to be repeated, Jenny. It's funny this time – but if it happens a second time, I shan't think it is at all funny. You quite understand that, don't you? White mice are very nice in their cage, but not at all suitable running round people's necks in a classroom.'

'Oh yes, I do understand that, Miss Ranger,' said Jenny earnestly. 'It was quite an accident. May I put the mouse up my sleeve again?'

'I'd much rather you didn't,' said Miss Ranger. 'I feel this lesson will not be very successful as long as that mouse is in the room. Take it back to its cage. It will have plenty to tell all its brothers and sisters.'

So off went Jenny, and the class settled down again. But the laughter had done everyone good, especially Elizabeth. She felt almost her old happy self again after that!

7 *Kathleen in trouble*

Elizabeth enjoyed the games in the winter term very much indeed. She didn't know which she liked best, hockey or lacrosse!

'I almost think I like lacrosse best,' she said to Joan. 'The catching is such fun.'

'If you go on playing well, you'll be in the next match,' said Joan. 'I heard Eileen say so!'

'Did you really and truly?' said Elizabeth joyfully. 'Oh, I say! Nobody else out of our form has been in a school match yet. If only I could be!'

Somebody else in the form was extremely good at lacrosse too – and that was Robert! He had never played the game before, but he was very quick on his feet, and could catch marvellously. The game was played with a hard rubber ball which had to be thrown from one player's net to another, caught, and sent hurtling at the goal-net. The job of the other side was to knock the ball away, or make the player who had the ball toss it to someone else, when the enemy might perhaps be able to get it.

As soon as Robert saw that Elizabeth was becoming good enough to play in a school match, he made up his mind that he would be better than she was, and take her place in the match.

He knew that only one person would be chosen from their form, for only one was lacking in the numbers that made up the team. What sport it would be if he could play better than Elizabeth! So that was another thing for him to do – practise catching the ball whenever he could get someone to throw to him. But he wouldn't let Elizabeth guess that he was trying to be better than she was – no, he would let her think he wasn't trying very hard, else she would begin to practise as well.

In the meantime, school life went on much as usual. Elizabeth began to work very hard with John in the school garden. They cut down all the old summer flowers, and piled them in heaps on the place where they had their bonfires. They dug over the beds, and made themselves very hot and tired but very happy. They each made out plans for the spring and gave them to each other, and John actually said that Elizabeth's plan was better than his.

'It's not very *much* better,' said John, looking at the two plans carefully, 'but I do like one or two of your ideas very much, Elizabeth. For instance, your idea of having crocuses growing in the grass on that bank over there is lovely.'

'Well, your idea of having rambler roses over that ugly old shed is lovely too,' said Elizabeth. 'I say, John, won't it look marvellous!'

'I wonder if the school Meeting will allow us extra money this week for the crocus corms,' said John. 'We should want about five hundred crocuses to make any sort of a show. Let's ask, shall we?'

'Well, *you'd* better ask, not me,' said Elizabeth, her face going sulky. 'You know what happened at the last Meeting, John. It was horrid to me.'

'No, it wasn't, Elizabeth,' said John, leaning on his spade and looking at Elizabeth across the trench he was digging. 'I think the Meeting was quite fair. Don't be silly. You can be such a sensible girl, and yet you're such an idiot some-times.'

'I shan't help you in the garden if you call me an idiot,' said Elizabeth.

'All right,' said John. 'I'll get Jenny. She's jolly good.'

But Elizabeth did not walk away in a rage as she felt inclined to do. She took up her spade and began to dig so hard that the earth simply flew into the air. She wasn't going to let Jennifer take her place!

John burst out laughing. 'Elizabeth! You'll dig down to Australia if you're not careful! And really I'd rather you didn't cover me with earth whilst you're doing it.'

Elizabeth looked up and laughed too.

'That's better!' said John. 'You'll get a face like Kathleen Peters if you aren't careful!'

'I hope not!' said Elizabeth. 'That's another person I don't like, John. She's so quarrelsome, and she seems to think we are always saying or thinking nasty things about her – and honestly, we just don't bother about her half the time.'

'Well, don't start making an enemy of her too,' said John, beginning to dig again. 'Friends are better than enemies, Elizabeth, old thing, so make those instead.'

'Well, nobody could make a friend of Kathleen!' said Elizabeth. 'Honestly they couldn't, John. You're not in her form, so you don't know what a tiresome person she is.'

It was quite true that Kathleen was tiresome.

She was always grumbling about something, and she spent the whole of her two pounds each week on sweets, which she never shared with anyone else.

'No wonder she's spotty!' giggled Belinda unkindly. 'She's eating sweets all the time – and her mother sends her heaps too, only she never tells us, in case we might expect her to share them. Let her keep them! I don't want any!'

Kathleen was not only tiresome with the boys and girls, always trying to quarrel, and accusing them of saying nasty things about her, but she was always in trouble with the mistresses and masters too. If anyone found fault with her, she would argue back and try to make out that she was right.

Mam'zelle was not so patient with her as were the others. When Kathleen dared to say that Mam'zelle hadn't told her what homework to do the day before, the hot-tempered French mistress flared up at once.

'And now, this Kathleen again!' she cried, wagging her hands at the ceiling. 'She thinks I am a goose, a cuckoo, a donkey! She thinks I do not know how to give homework! She thinks I am not fit to teach French to her!'

This was really rather funny, and the class sat up, enjoying the fun. When Mam'zelle got cross it was marvellous!

'But, Mam'zelle,' said foolish Kathleen, who simply would not stop arguing with anyone, 'you did say . . .'

'Ah! I did say something then!' cried Mam'zelle. 'Truly, you think I did say something? Ah, my Kathleen, that is so, so kind of you! Perhaps if you think a little harder you will remember that I did give you some homework to do – though, of course, that is no reason why you should do it.'

'But you DIDN'T give me any,' said Kathleen.

Belinda nudged her. 'Shut up, Kathleen,' she said. 'You *were* given some – but you didn't write down what you had to do.'

'Belinda! It is not necessary that you should interfere,' said Mam'zelle. 'Ah, this class! It will turn my hair white as snow!'

Mam'zelle had hair as dark as a raven's wing, and the class did not feel that anything would turn it white. They sat staring from Mam'zelle to Kathleen, wondering what was going to happen next. It ended in Kathleen being sent by herself to the common room to do the homework she had not done.

'That girl will drive me mad,' thought Mam'zelle to herself, 'with her spots and her greasy hair and pale face. How she whines!'

The other mistresses were not quite so impatient, and Miss Ranger was really rather worried about Kathleen. The girl always looked so miserable – which, of course, was no wonder, because she was always arguing or quarrelling with someone.

Jennifer Harris enjoyed the scene with Mam'zelle very much. She watched all Mam'zelle's actions, listened carefully to the rise and fall of her excited voice, and then practised the whole scene by herself. First she was the whining Kathleen, then she was impatient Mam'zelle, and so on. It really made a very funny scene.

Jenny was most anxious to try it on the others to make them laugh. So the next evening, when most of her form were in the common-room, playing the gramophone, reading books, and writing letters, she began to mimic Mam'zelle.

The boys and girls looked up, interested. Belinda switched off the gramophone. Kathleen was not there.

In a moment or two the clever girl had the whole room roaring with laughter. She wagged her hands like Mam'zelle, and when she came out with 'I am a goose, a cuckoo, a donkey!' exactly as Mam'zelle had said it, the children giggled in delight.

Jenny mimicked Kathleen's rather whining voice marvellously. It really might have been Kathleen speaking! But then Jenny went a bit too far. She said things that Mam'zelle had not said.

'Ah, truly, Kathleen, I do not like your spots, I do not like your greasy hair, I do not like your manners!' said Jenny, with a funny accent just like Mam'zelle's. And at that moment Elizabeth noticed something – Kathleen was in the room! No one had seen her come in. How long had she been there?

Elizabeth nudged Jenny, but Jenny took no notice. She was enjoying herself far too much. Everyone was listening to her, amused and admiring.

'Jenny! Shut up!' hissed Elizabeth. 'Kathleen's come in.'

Jenny stopped at once. All the children looked round, and felt rather uncomfortable when they saw Kathleen. Belinda started up the gramophone. Somebody began to whistle the tune. Nobody liked to look at Kathleen.

Elizabeth sat down in a corner, wishing that Jenny hadn't said quite such awful things in Mam'zelle's voice. Suppose Kathleen really thought that Mam'zelle had said them after she had been sent to the common room to do her forgotten homework? She stole a quick look at Kathleen.

At first it seemed as if Kathleen was going to turn off the gramophone and say something. But she thought better of it, and sat down with a jerk in a chair. She got out her notepaper, and sat chewing the end of her pen. Her pale face was as white as usual, and her eyes were small and angry. She looked spiteful and mean.

'I guess she won't easily forgive Jenny for that,' thought Elizabeth. 'We ought to have stopped Jenny, because she went too far – but really, she's so awfully funny. I wonder if Kathleen will complain about it at the next Meeting. I shouldn't be surprised.'

Kathleen didn't say a word about the affair to anyone. She spoke to no one at all that evening. Her bed was next to Elizabeth's in the dormitory, and when Kathleen did not reply when everyone called goodnight as usual, Elizabeth poked her head between the white curtains to speak to her, for she was sorry about the whole thing.

Kathleen did not see her. The girl was sitting on her bed, looking earnestly at her face in her hand-mirror. She looked really sad, and Elizabeth knew why. Poor Kathleen was thinking how plain and ugly she was! She had always known it herself – but it was dreadful to know that everyone else knew it too, and laughed about it.

Elizabeth drew back her head and said nothing. Would Kathleen have the courage to repeat at the Meeting all that Jenny had said about her? Surely she couldn't do that!

Kathleen had her own plans. She was going to pay Jenny out in her own way. She got into bed and lay thinking about them. Jenny had better look out, that's all!

8 Another school Meeting

Things were not very pleasant the next two or three days. There seemed to be rather a lot of bad feeling about. For one thing, Kathleen simply would not speak to Jenny at all, which was not very surprising considering what she had overheard Jenny saying.

But besides not speaking to her, Kathleen began to speak *against* her. Jenny was always very hungry, and she ate very well indeed – and Kathleen called her greedy.

'It makes me sick to see the way that greedy Jenny eats,' she said to Belinda, after tea the next day. 'Honestly, she ate seven pieces of bread-and-butter, and three buns, besides an enormous piece of birthday cake that Harriet gave her.'

Belinda said nothing. She did not like rows – but Elizabeth overheard and flared up at once in defence of Jenny.

'That's a mean thing to say, Kathleen!' she said. 'Jenny *isn't* greedy! She's always terribly hungry at mealtimes – well, I am too, I must say – but I've never seen Jenny gobbling just for the sake of eating, or taking more than her share if there wasn't enough for everyone. And how awful of you to *count* how many pieces of bread-and-butter she had!'

'I shall count again,' said Kathleen, 'and you'll be surprised to find I'm right. Jenny is greedy. It's disgusting!'

'Kathleen! What about you and your sweets then!' cried Elizabeth. 'You're greedy over them – why, you never offer anyone any!'

'Stop it now, you two,' said Belinda, feeling uncomfortable. 'I don't know what's the matter with our form this term – somebody always seems to be quarrelling!'

Kathleen went off. Elizabeth took out her paint-box to paint a map, and set it down on the table with a crash. Her face was as black as thunder.

'Elizabeth! I wonder you haven't broken that box in half!' exclaimed Belinda. 'My word, I wish you could see your face!'

'I think you might have stuck up for Jenny,' said Elizabeth, stirring her paint water so crossly that it slopped over on the table. 'I wouldn't let anyone say a word against a friend of mine without sticking up for them.'

'Well, you've made things much worse by sticking up, than I have by saying nothing,' said Belinda. 'I don't know what's come over you lately – you're really bad-tempered!'

'No, I'm not,' said Elizabeth. 'Things have gone wrong, that's all. Anyway, I won't let that spotty-faced Kathleen say mean things about old Jenny. Jenny's a sport. Golly, how I laughed about that white mouse the other day! Miss Ranger was nice about that, wasn't she?'

About a quarter of an hour later, Jenny came into the common room looking furious. She sat down in a chair with a bump. Belinda looked up from her sewing.

'My goodness! Another thunderstorm beginning!' she said. 'What's up, Jenny? One look at you and even the milk would turn sour!'

'Don't be funny,' said Jenny. 'It's that horrible Kathleen! She told Kenneth that I borrowed his bike yesterday without asking him. And I didn't. I took Harry's and I *did* ask him! Mine had a puncture!'

'Well, really, Kathleen's going a bit too far!' said Elizabeth indignantly. 'That's twice she's said nasty things about you today. I'll tell her what I think of her when I see her!'

'She's in the passage outside, still telling Kenneth about me,' said Jenny. 'Go and say what you want to – it will do her good!'

'No, don't, Elizabeth,' said Belinda. 'You are such a little spitfire. Don't interfere.'

But Elizabeth had already marched out of the room. She saw Kathleen and went up to her.

'Look here, Kathleen,' she said, 'if you don't stop saying unkind and untrue things about Jenny, I'll report you to the next Meeting!'

'And what about the unkind and untrue things that Jenny said about me in front of you all!' said Kathleen in a low and trembling voice. 'How dared she mock me like that!'

'Well, they might have been unkind, but they weren't untrue,' said Elizabeth. Then she was sorry she had said that. But it was too late to unsay it. Kathleen turned away and went off without saying another word.

She was really afraid that Elizabeth might report her, and she made up her mind that she had better not speak against Jenny. But she would do all kinds of little things to annoy her and get her into trouble – and she would do them to that interfering Elizabeth, too.

'I'll be very, very careful so that nobody guesses

it's me,' thought Kathleen to herself. 'I'll hide their books – and make blots on their homework – and do things like that. I'll soon pay them out!'

The next school Meeting came along quickly. The children took their places as usual, and the Meeting began. A nice lot of money was put into the box, for three children had had birthdays and had many postal orders sent to them. That was lucky!

'We are rich today,' said William, jingling the box. 'Give out the ordinary money, Eileen – and twenty pence extra to Mary as usual. Now – any requests for extra money?'

Leonard, one of the bigger boys, stood up. 'May I have five pounds to pay for mending a window, please?' he asked. 'I broke one yesterday in the common room.'

'By accident, or were you fooling about?' asked William.

'I was playing with an old cricket ball,' said Leonard.

'Well, you know quite well that we made a rule last term not to bring balls into the common room,' said William. 'It only means broken windows.'

'I quite forgot that rule,' said Leonard. 'I *should* like the money, though – five pounds is a lot to have to pay. I'm sorry about it, William.'

The Jury discussed the matter. They quite saw that five pounds was a lot of money when each boy and girl only had two pounds each week. On the other hand, Leonard had broken a rule that he himself had helped to make last term, and why should the school money pay for his fooling about?

The matter was decided at last. William banged with his hammer and the children were quiet.

'Was anybody else fooling about with you?' asked William. Leonard stood up again.

'Well, yes,' he said, 'but it was when *I* threw the ball that the window got broken.'

'The Jury think that the five pounds shouldn't come out of the school box,' said William, 'but they also think that you shouldn't have to pay it all. You'd better discuss it with the children who were playing about with you at the time, and divide the payment between you. That's fair.'

A boy got up. 'I was fooling about too,' he said. 'I'll pay my share. I agree that it's fair.'

Two others got up, a boy and a girl. 'We will pay our share too,' they said.

'Right,' said William. 'Four into five pounds – one pound twenty five pence each. That won't ruin any of you. And please remember that as you all help to make the few rules we have, it's up to you to keep them.'

John nudged Elizabeth. 'Ask for the money for our crocuses,' he whispered. 'Go on. I'm not going to! It was your idea.'

'I'm sure the Meeting won't let me have anything after what they said last week,' said Elizabeth in a fierce whisper.

'Coward!' said John, with a grin. That was quite enough to make Elizabeth shoot to her feet at once. She could never bear to be called a coward!

Kathleen looked at her rather anxiously. She was half afraid that Elizabeth was going to complain about her to the Meeting.

'What do you want, Elizabeth?' asked Rita. 'Extra money?'

'Yes, please,' said Elizabeth. 'John and I have got some fine plans for the school garden and we both think it would be lovely to have yellow and purple crocuses growing in the grass on that sloping bank near the gates. John says we'd want at least five hundred crocus bulbs. Please may we have the money to buy them, Rita?'

William and Rita spoke together for a moment and the Jury nodded their heads at one another.

Everyone thought the money could be given.

'Yes, you can have what you want,' said William. 'The whole school will enjoy seeing the crocuses in the early spring, and it is quite fair that the money should come out of the school box. Find out how much the bulbs will be, Elizabeth, and we shall be very pleased to give you the money. Also, I would like to say that the whole school appreciates the way that you and John work at our garden.'

Elizabeth blushed with pleasure. This was quite unexpected. She sat down with a word of thanks. John grinned in delight at her. 'What did I tell you?' he whispered. 'You can always trust William and Rita to be absolutely fair!'

'Any complaints or grumbles?' asked Rita. A small boy got up promptly. He was a cheeky-looking child, and had his complaint all ready.

'I should like to make a complaint about Fred White,' he said. 'He's always borrowing my things and never giving them back.'

'That's telling a tale, not making a proper complaint,' said William at once. 'Go to your monitor to decide silly little things of that sort. Who is your monitor?'

'I am,' said a boy called Thomas.

'Well, please explain carefully the difference between telling tales and making a genuine complaint,' said William. 'We only decide serious things at this Meeting.'

'Any more complaints?' asked Rita. A boy called William Peace got up. He was in the form below Elizabeth, a serious-faced boy.

'I have a small complaint to make,' he said. 'I learn the violin and I see that my practice-times have been altered to the times when my form goes for a Nature ramble. I belong to the Nature Society, and I hate to miss the rambles. May the time of one of them be altered?'

'It would be quite easy,' said William. 'Discuss it with Mr Lewis, the music-master, and see if there is anyone who can change practice-times with you.'

'Thank you,' said the boy, and sat down. There were no more complaints. Kathleen did not get up and say anything at all, though the others in her form were almost sure that she would complain about Jenny. They did not know that the girl was going to punish Jenny in her own way.

'The Meeting is dismissed,' said William, and the school filed out, chattering as soon as the

children got to their various common-rooms.
Elizabeth went to John.

'It's good that we can have the money for the
crocuses, isn't it?' she said, with her eyes shining.
'We'll go down to the town tomorrow, John, and
see how much they are. I'm longing to plant them,
aren't you? October is the right month. They will
look so lovely in the springtime.'

'Elizabeth, I wish you knew how much nicer
you look when you are all happy and smiling like
that,' said John. 'It is so horrid when you frown
and sulk.'

'You're always lecturing me, John!' said
Elizabeth. But she was glad all the same that
John was pleased with her. Alas! He was not
going to be pleased with her for long!

9 Kathleen plays some tricks

Kathleen did not change her mind about paying back Elizabeth and Jenny. She began to play all kinds of mean little tricks on them, and she played them so cleverly that they did not guess she had done them.

She slipped into the classroom after tea when there was no one there and went to Jenny's desk. She knew that Jenny had written out her French homework very carefully indeed, and she had seen her put the book back into her desk.

Kathleen took out the book and opened it at the place where the work had been done. She dipped a pen in the ink – and then she made three large blots on the page by shaking the pen hard!

She looked at it. The page was dreadful. Jenny would get into trouble, no doubt about that! She waited until the blots were dry and then shut the book. She slipped it into the desk and ran back to the common room. She saw Jenny there and gave her a sly look. 'Ah, wait, Jenny! You'll have a shock tomorrow,' thought Kathleen.

Elizabeth was in the room too, putting one of her favourite gramophone records on. Kathleen wondered what she could do to her. She sat and thought for a while, then quietly got up. She slipped out of the room and put on her coat. It was dark outside, and she went out of the garden door into the school grounds.

She went to where Elizabeth kept her spade, fork, and trowels. John always insisted that every tool used should be cleaned till it was bright and shining, before it was put away. Elizabeth was always particular about this, for she knew that well-kept tools did good work.

Kathleen took down the garden tools. She carried them outside, and went to a place where she knew that the earth was damp and muddy. She dug the tools into the wet soil and made them very dirty indeed.

Then she carried them back to the shed and put them into a corner. She shone her torch on to them. They were brown with mud. John would be furious when he found them – and as they were the ones that Elizabeth always used, he would be sure to think that she had been careless.

'Well, I'll soon teach Jenny and Elizabeth that

it doesn't pay to be horrid to me!' thought Kathleen to herself, as she went back to take off her coat. 'They deserve to be punished! They've been mean to me. Now I'm being mean back to them. Serves them right!'

She went back to the common room. She couldn't help feeling rather victorious somehow, and she longed for the next day to come, so that she might see her two enemies getting into trouble.

The first one to get into trouble was poor Jenny. Mam'zelle asked Kenneth to collect the French books and Jenny gave hers up without even opening it. Mam'zelle set the class some translation to do, and then opened the French exercise books to correct them.

When she came to Jenny's and saw the three enormous blots across the page, blotting out some of the sentences, she threw up her hands in horror.

'What is this?' she cried. 'Whose book is this?' She looked quickly at the name, and gazed across at Jenny in astonishment.

'Jennifer Harris! How can you give in work like this! It is shocking!'

Jenny looked up in surprise. What *could* be the matter with her work? She had done it quite carefully. 'Why, Mam'zelle!' she said. 'Is there something wrong?'

'Jenny, my child, you do not belong to the kindergarten!' cried Mam'zelle, holding up the book for Jenny to see. 'Look at this page! Is it not disgraceful? You know that you should have written out all this work again – work from this form cannot be given in covered with blots. I am truly ashamed of you!'

Jenny stared in the greatest surprise at her book. She knew quite well she hadn't made any blots at all. It couldn't be her book!

'That's not my book, Mam'zelle,' she said. 'It can't be. I didn't make any blots at all. I would never give in work like that.'

'Jenny, I am not blind as a bat!' cried Mam'zelle, beginning to get excited. 'I read your name here, see – Jennifer Harris. It is most certainly your book. And if you did not make these blots, how did they come? Blots do not make themselves, as you very well know.'

'I simply can't imagine how they came,' said poor Jenny, really puzzled now. 'Honestly I can't, Mam'zelle, I'm most awfully sorry. I'll do the work again.'

'And you will be more careful in future,' said

Mam'zelle, calming down. Jenny was upset and puzzled. She supposed that in some way she must have made the blots without noticing them, just as she shut the book. She did not see Kathleen looking at her with a spiteful gleam in her eyes. Kathleen was delighted at the success of her trick. She would play a few more on Jenny very soon!

There was half an hour that afternoon for any child to go for a walk, practise lacrosse, or do gardening. Elizabeth chose to go to the garden. There was one piece she hadn't quite been able to finish digging the day before. She could just finish it in the time.

So off she skipped, and called out to John who was already digging hard. But John did not look at all pleased with her.

'Elizabeth, you did do some digging and forking yesterday, didn't you?' he called.

'Rather!' said Elizabeth, stopping beside him. 'I used nearly all my tools, I was so busy. What's the matter, John? You look cross.'

'I *am* cross,' said John. 'Go and get your tools and you'll see why.'

Elizabeth couldn't *think* what he meant. She rushed off to the shed – and stopped in surprise and dismay when she saw her tools. They were all muddy and dirty! Not one of them shone bright and silvery. What a very extraordinary thing!

She went outside, carrying them with her. 'John!' she said. 'I'm quite sure I cleaned them as usual yesterday when I put them away.'

'You can't have,' said John in a cold sort of voice. 'Tools don't get dirty at night by themselves, Elizabeth. Have some sense.'

'I've got plenty!' cried Elizabeth. 'And my sense tells me that if I *did* clean them, which I know I did, it's not *my* fault that they're dirty now.'

'Well, don't let's argue about it,' said John. 'I'd have thought a lot more of you, Elizabeth, if you'd owned up, and said you'd forgotten just for once. It's not like you to say you did a thing, when you didn't.'

'John!' cried Elizabeth, shocked. 'How can you say such a thing about me! I'm never afraid of owning up. You know that. I tell you I *did* clean the tools.'

'All right, all right,' said John, going on with the digging. 'I suppose they all walked out of the shed in the middle of the night and went digging by themselves and forgot to have a wash and brush-up afterwards. We'll leave it at that.'

The two children dug in silence. Elizabeth was puzzled, upset, and angry. She hated to think that John didn't believe her, and yet her common sense told her that it really did look as if she had forgotten to clean her tools. It was horrid to have John cross with her. She didn't know what to do.

'John,' she said at last, 'I really do think I cleaned the tools, but if I forgot, I'm very sorry. I've never forgotten before. I won't forget again.'

'All right, Elizabeth,' said John, lifting his honest brown eyes to hers. He smiled at her, and she smiled back. But in her secret heart she was very puzzled indeed.

Kathleen had been waiting about by the garden shed to see what would happen. She was pleased when she saw that John was cross with Elizabeth. She went away, planning to do something else to get Elizabeth into trouble. What should she do next? Perhaps in a day or two she would dirty the tools again. She had better not do that too soon, though, in case Elizabeth began to suspect a trick.

She decided to take two or three of Elizabeth's books and hide them somewhere. Miss Ranger would be cross if they couldn't be found. So once again Kathleen slipped into the classroom, and this time she went to Elizabeth's desk. She took out her geography exercise book, her arithmetic book, and her history book. She slipped out of the room with them and went to a cupboard outside. On the top were kept old maps. Kathleen stood on a chair and threw the books right on the very top, among the old maps. Nobody was about to see her. She quickly put back the chair, and went away.

And now, what should she do to Jenny? The naughty girl frowned, and thought hard. Then she smiled to herself. She would take two of the white mice and put them into Miss Ranger's desk! That would be marvellous! Miss Ranger would be quite sure to think that Jenny had put them there herself. Nobody would know who had done it.

To do this Kathleen had to wait till the next morning. She planned to get the mice before breakfast. No one would be about then. She lay in bed that night thinking of what Miss Ranger would say when she opened the desk and found the mice.

She was up early the next morning. Nora was surprised, for Kathleen was usually one of the last out of bed. 'Hallo, turning over a new leaf?' she said.

Kathleen didn't answer. She slipped downstairs five minutes before the breakfast-bell went, and ran to the big shed where the pets were kept. She went to the cage of white mice. She had with her a little box, and it took her only a second or two to pick up two of the tiny white mice and slip them into the box. Then she hurried to her classroom with them. She lifted up the lid of Miss Ranger's desk.

She opened the box – and out scurried the white mice into the desk. Kathleen shut down the lid. What a surprise Miss Ranger and Jenny were going to get!

10 Excitement in class!

The first lesson that morning was arithmetic. Miss Ranger explained a new kind of sum to the class, and they listened hard.

'Now get out your books and we will do a few of these sums,' said Miss Ranger, beginning to put down a few on the blackboard. 'You should all be able to do them correctly, but if anyone hasn't quite understood what I have been saying, ask me first, before you begin the sums.'

Elizabeth opened her desk to get out her arithmetic exercise book. It wasn't on the top of the pile, where she usually put it. She hunted through her desk. How funny! The book wasn't there at all. Where could it be?

'Elizabeth! How much longer are you going to have your head in your desk?' asked Miss Ranger.

'I can't find my book,' said Elizabeth.

'Well, you had it yesterday,' said Miss Ranger. 'Did you take it out of the classroom?'

'No, Miss Ranger,' said Elizabeth. 'I hadn't any

arithmetic homework to do. I just put the book back when I'd finished with it yesterday morning. But it really isn't here.'

'Take some squared paper from the shelf in the cupboard,' said Miss Ranger. 'We can't wait all morning for you to find the book.' So Elizabeth took some squared paper and did her sums on that, thankful that she hadn't got into trouble. She simply could *not* imagine where her book could be! She kept on and on thinking about it.

Kathleen wondered what would happen when Elizabeth couldn't find the other books! She was also longing for Miss Ranger to open her own desk and find the mice. But Miss Ranger had no reason to open her desk in the arithmetic lesson. So the mice remained undisturbed. They had curled up in a corner and gone to sleep.

The next lesson was French, and after that came geography. Miss Ranger wanted a map drawn, and the girls got out their exercise books. And once again Elizabeth couldn't find hers.

'Well, really, Elizabeth, you are surely not going to tell me that your geography book is lost, too!' said Miss Ranger impatiently.

'Miss Ranger, I just can't understand it, but it's gone,' said Elizabeth, putting her head above the desk-lid to speak to Miss Ranger.

'It is very careless of you to lose both books,' said Miss Ranger. 'I am not pleased, Elizabeth. Perhaps I had better look through your desk myself to make quite sure that they are not there. I can't imagine that you could lose *two* of your exercise books, when you say you did not even take them out of the classroom!'

But not even Miss Ranger's sharp eye could see the missing books, and she went back to her own desk. Robert was pleased to see Elizabeth getting into trouble. As for Kathleen, she was so delighted at the success of her mean trick that she did not dare to look at either Elizabeth or Jenny in case they saw how glad she was.

'I will give you some map-paper, and you must pin the map you draw into your book, when it is found again,' said Miss Ranger. She lifted up the lid of her desk to get some blank drawing-paper – and awoke the two mice!

With squeals and squeaks they raced round the desk in fright, jumping over rubbers and books and rulers. Miss Ranger stared at them in amazement and anger.

She was about to shut down the desk and leave the mice there, when they both leapt out, ran down Miss Ranger's skirt and tore across the floor. All the girls and boys stared in the greatest astonishment.

Miss Ranger put on a very stern face and looked at the surprised Jenny.

'Jenny,' she said, 'I believe you are the only person in the school who keeps white mice as pets. Do you really think it is a funny joke to put the poor little things into my airless desk in order to play a foolish trick on me?'

Jenny couldn't say a word at first. She really was too amazed to speak. *Were* they her mice? How in the world could they have got into the desk?

'Miss Ranger, of *course* I didn't put them in there!' she said at last. 'Please, please believe me. I wouldn't do such a thing to my little mice. And anyway, you were so decent to me when I came to class with one down my neck that I certainly wouldn't have been mean enough to play a trick on you after that.'

The mice fled all over the room. Jenny watched them anxiously, terrified that they would go under the door and escape – perhaps to get eaten by the school cat!

'You had better try to catch them,' said Miss

Ranger. 'We can't have the whole lesson disturbed like this. I can't imagine how they could have got into my desk unless you put them there. I shall have to think about the whole thing. I am very displeased about it.'

Jenny leapt up from her seat to catch the mice. But that was easier said than done. The frightened creatures tore all over the room, hiding under first one desk and then another. Some of the girls pretended to be frightened and squealed whenever a mouse came near to their feet. Elizabeth and Belinda tried to help, but those mice were too nimble to be caught.

And then, to Jenny's great dismay, they squeezed themselves under the schoolroom door, and escaped into the passage outside! Jenny ran to the door and opened it – but the mice had disappeared! Goodness knew where they had gone! The little girl ran down the passage, looking everywhere, but the mice were nowhere to be seen.

Jenny was really fond of her mice. Tears came into her eyes and she brushed them away. But others came, and she did not like to go back to the classroom crying. So she leaned against the passage wall for a minute, trying to fight back her tears. Someone had played a mean trick on her! Someone had tried to get her into trouble! Someone had made her lose two of her pets! It was horrid, horrid, horrid!

Footsteps came down the passage – and who should come round the corner but Rita, the head girl! She was most surprised to see Jenny standing there, crying.

'What's the matter?' she asked. 'Have you been sent out of the room?'

'No,' said poor Jenny. 'It's my white mice. They're gone – and I'm so afraid the school cat will eat them.' She poured out the whole story to Rita. The head girl looked very grave.

'I don't like the idea of somebody trying to get you into trouble like this,' she said. 'You are quite, quite sure you didn't play the trick yourself, Jenny?'

'Oh, Rita – I really couldn't treat my pets like that,' said Jenny earnestly. 'Do believe me.'

'Well, the matter must be brought up at the next Meeting,' said Rita. 'We'll have to get to the bottom of it. Now go back to your class, Jenny. Cheer up. Maybe the mice will turn up again!'

Jenny went back. Miss Ranger saw her red eyes and did not scold her any more. The bell went for the lesson to stop, and the class put away their books. Break came next. Thank goodness!

Robert bumped into Elizabeth as they went out of the classroom, and she glared at him. 'How many more books are you going to lose?' he asked.

Elizabeth tossed her head and walked off with Joan. But a thought came into her head. Could Robert have taken her books? It really was so very extraordinary that both her arithmetic book *and* her geography book should have gone! She went over to Jenny and pulled her into a corner.

'Do you think Robert has got anything to do with my losing my books and your mice being put into the desk?' she said. 'I know he'd like to get me into trouble.'

'Yes – but why should he get *me* into trouble, too?' said Jenny.

'Oh, he might think that if he played tricks only on *me*, I would guess it was him,' said Elizabeth. 'But if he played tricks on you and anybody else, we might not think it was him at all. See?'

'Well, he must be pretty horrid if he's as mean as all that,' said Jenny, troubled. 'Oh, Elizabeth, I wish I knew who it was. It's so awful having these things happen.'

It was even more horrid when the history lesson came and Elizabeth had to confess to Miss Ranger that that book had disappeared too!

'Elizabeth! This is really peculiar,' said Miss Ranger crossly. 'One book is enough to lose – but *three*! You must have taken them out of the classroom and left them somewhere. You must hunt for them well, and if you cannot find them you must come to me and buy new ones.'

'Oh, bother!' thought Elizabeth in dismay. 'They are fifty pence each. That's one fifty out of my precious two pounds. It's too bad! If Robert has hidden my books I'll pull all the hairs out of his head!'

She said this to Joan. 'No, you won't do anything of the sort,' said Joan. 'You'll report him at the Meeting and let the school judge him. After all, that's what the Meeting is for, Elizabeth – for all of us to help to untangle the difficulties of a few of us. It's much better, too, to let the Jury and the Judges decide for us, because we have chosen them as being the wisest among us. Don't take matters into your own hands, Elizabeth. You're such an impatient person – you'll only do something silly!'

'I wish you wouldn't keep talking to me like

that,' said Elizabeth, taking her arm from Joan's. 'You might back me up!'

'I *am* backing you up, if you only knew it,' said Joan with a sigh. 'I would be a poor friend to you if I said, "Go to Robert and pull his hair out," even before you really know for certain whether he is playing these horrid tricks, or not.'

'Well, you've only got to see how pleased he is when I get into trouble to know that he's at the bottom of it all!' cried Elizabeth. 'Oh, if only I could catch him bullying someone again. Wouldn't I love to report him at the very next Meeting!'

Elizabeth hadn't long to wait. She caught Robert the very next day!

11 More trouble

For some time now Robert had not bullied anyone or been unkind, because he really had been afraid of being seen by Elizabeth. He knew that she was watching to catch him and he did not mean to give her any chance to report him again.

But two or three weeks had now gone by and he thought that she no longer bothered to watch. He did not know that she thought he had played the tricks on her and was watching very carefully indeed.

Robert had to go and get some water for his painting after tea. Elizabeth saw him go out of the common room and she looked at Joan.

'Joan! Do you think Robert has gone to take my books again, or do some horrid trick?' she said in a low voice. 'Let's follow him and see.'

So the two girls got up and followed Robert. He went down the passage, and ran down the stairs to the cloakroom where the water taps were. And running round the corner came small, cheeky Leslie, the boy who had complained that another was always borrowing things and not giving them back. He ran full-tilt into Robert, and made him double up in pain.

Leslie giggled. It was funny to see big Robert panting like that! Robert put out a hand and caught him, holding the boy's arm so tightly that it hurt.

'Let me go,' said Leslie.

Robert looked up and down the passage quickly. No one was about. He pulled Leslie into the wash-place and shook him hard.

'How dare you run into me like that!' he demanded. 'And I'll teach you to laugh at me, you little nuisance!'

'Robert, let me go!' begged Leslie again. He knew that Robert was a bully and he was afraid of him.

'Say "I humbly beg your pardon, and I will never, never do such a thing again!" ' said Robert.

But Leslie, although he was afraid, was not a coward. He shook his head. 'I'm not going to be as humble as all that!' he said. 'You let me go, you big bully!'

Robert was angry. He shook Leslie hard again.

'You say what I told you to say, or I'll make you sit on the hot-water pipes!' he said.

Hot-water pipes ran all round the wash-place to warm it. Leslie glanced at them fearfully. But he still shook his head.

'No, I shan't beg your pardon,' he said obstinately. 'If you'd been decent to me, as any other of the big boys would have been, I'd have said I was sorry like a shot. Let me go!'

'You'll sit on the hot-water pipes first!' said Robert in a rage, and he dragged poor Leslie towards the pipes. They were not terribly hot, but hot enough to make Leslie shout.

Meantime, where were Elizabeth and Joan? They were just round the corner, listening to all that was said, and when they heard Robert pulling Leslie to the hot pipes they ran into the wash-place at once. Leslie was just shouting.

Robert pulled the little boy off the pipes as soon as he saw Elizabeth and Joan. He went red and looked very angry. To think he had been caught by those interfering girls – and one of them Elizabeth too!

'We've caught you nicely, you horrid boy,' said Elizabeth scornfully. 'Leslie, we are going to report Robert at the next Meeting. Just see you tell the truth and back us up in what we say.'

'I'll do that all right,' said Leslie. 'I'm not a little coward like some of the others, who didn't dare to complain about Robert when they had the chance! As for Peter, you know why *he* didn't say that Robert was swinging him much too high, don't you? Robert went to him and threatened him with all kinds of punishment if he dared to say a word against him!'

'I did not,' said Robert angrily, though he knew perfectly well that what Leslie said was true. 'You wait till I get you alone again, that's all!'

'There you are, you see!' said Leslie. 'You would like to do exactly the same thing to me again. But you won't get the chance! I'll report you at the Meeting all right, even if Elizabeth and Joan don't!'

The small boy marched off. Elizabeth turned to Robert. She spoke fiercely. 'I know jolly well that it's you that has been playing those horrid tricks on me and on Jenny,' she said.

'I did not,' said Robert, this time speaking quite truthfully.

'Well, I don't believe you!' said Elizabeth. 'You are mean enough for anything. You're a perfectly horrid boy and I think you ought to be sent away from our school.'

'Just as *you* ought to have been sent away last term, I suppose!' said Robert mockingly. He had heard all about Elizabeth's naughtiness during the summer term. Elizabeth went red.

'Be quiet!' said Joan. 'It was a good deal because Elizabeth wanted to be kind to *me* that she was disobedient and I won't have you sneering at her for that!'

'I shall say what I like,' said Robert, and went off by himself, hands in pockets, whistling as if he didn't care about anything at all.

'Well, now that he knows we know he played those nasty tricks, he won't dare to play any more,' said Elizabeth, pleased. 'So that's something!'

But, of course, it was Kathleen who had tried to get Elizabeth and Jenny into trouble, not Robert – and she saw no reason why she should stop being horrid to the two girls whom she so much disliked. Both girls were pretty, clever, and amusing – three things that poor Kathleen was not – and she was jealous of their shining hair and bright eyes, their good brains and jolly jokes. She wanted to hurt the girls who had the things she hadn't and yet so much wanted to have.

Elizabeth told Jenny that she was sure it was Robert who had taken her mice, and put them in the desk. The mice had never been found again and Jenny had been sad ever since. Her eyes flashed when she heard Elizabeth say that it was Robert who had played the trick.

'And I suppose he blotted my French book too, so that I had to do the work again!' said Jenny angrily. 'And I shouldn't be surprised if he dirtied those garden tools of yours, Elizabeth – I could never understand that, you know.'

'Well, I guess we shan't have any more tricks played on us, because Robert will be afraid we'll tell them all to the Meeting,' said Elizabeth. 'And we will too!'

But next day another trick was played on her and on Jenny too. On Wednesdays their monitor had to look at all their drawers and their hanging-cupboards to see that they were tidy. Nora was very strict about tidiness, and the girls in her dormitory had learnt to be very neat indeed – even Ruth, who was most untidy by nature, and found it difficult to keep any drawer neat.

'It's awful!' she complained about three times a week. 'I tidy my drawers so well – then I want a handkerchief in a hurry and can't find it, and turn the drawer upside down, and then it's all untidy again!'

Elizabeth and Jenny were quite tidy, and they always made a rule on Tuesday night to tidy everything beautifully so that their chest and cupboard were ready for Nora to inspect the next day. They had done this as usual – so on Wednesday, when Nora went to pull open their drawers and found everything in a most terrible muddle, they were too astonished to say anything.

'Jenny! Elizabeth! What *have* you been thinking of to get your things into such a disgraceful mess!' cried Nora, looking at their drawers. 'Look – everything jumbled up – crumpled, untidy – honestly I've never seen such a mess. And you are usually so tidy, both of you. What have you been doing? Didn't you remember I always looked on Wednesdays?'

'Of course we remembered,' said Jenny. 'And we tidied them last night before we went to bed. Why, you must have noticed us, Nora.'

'I didn't notice,' said Nora. 'I was at the other end of the dormitory.'

The three girls looked into the drawers. Everything was upside down. Elizabeth and Jenny knew perfectly they could never have got their things into that muddle. Somebody had played a hateful trick again, to get them into trouble.

'It's Robert!' burst out Elizabeth. 'He's always playing horrid jokes on us, Nora. He dirtied my tools, and took my books, and put Jenny's mice into Miss Ranger's desk, and . . .'

'My dear girl, it couldn't have been Robert who did this,' said Nora. 'You know the boys never come into this part of the school. He would have been seen at once, because there is always somebody going up and down the passage outside.'

'Well, it must have been Robert,' said Elizabeth sulkily. 'If you're going to get anyone into trouble, for these untidy drawers, Nora, you ought to go and scold Robert.'

'I'm not going to scold anyone,' said Nora. 'You're neither of you so untidy as all that! I think someone *has* been mean to you. Anyway, tidy your things, for goodness' sake.'

The girls set to work. They were both angry. They did not notice how pleased Kathleen looked. 'Ah,' she thought, 'so Elizabeth and Jenny thought that it was Robert who had played tricks! Good!' Nobody would think it was she, Kathleen, who had done them all. She felt much safer now.

The next school Meeting was not until Friday night. On Thursday something happened that disappointed Elizabeth very much. The Lacrosse Match was to be on Saturday, and she had been practising very hard indeed to be good enough to play in it. Only one of her form was to be chosen for the school team, and Elizabeth felt certain she would be the one.

But when she went to look at the notice-board, on which were pinned notices of matches, rambles, and so on, she found that Robert's name was set down for the match instead of hers!

There it was – 'Robert Jones has been chosen from Form One to play in the Lacrosse Match on Saturday against Kinellan School.'

There was a lump in Elizabeth's throat. She had tried so hard! She did so badly want to play. She was very good, really she was! And now that horrid, hateful Robert had been chosen instead of her. She could really hardly believe it.

'Never mind,' said Joan. 'You'll get a chance next time, I expect.'

'I *do* mind!' said Elizabeth fiercely. 'He will crow over me now. Oh, how I hope that the school Meeting will punish him well and say he's not to play in the match!'

Robert was delighted to see his name down, but for all his pleasure he was really very anxious indeed. He knew Elizabeth and Joan were going to report him at the Meeting and he was not looking forward to that. He was a little coward at heart, and he was afraid.

So when Friday came, Robert looked rather anxious. If only the Meeting were after Saturday, so that he could play in the match first! How marvellous that he had been chosen and not Elizabeth! Serve her right, the interfering girl!

The time for the Meeting came. The children took their places, looking rather solemn, for they knew it was going to be a serious one.

12 A very serious Meeting

Even the smaller children felt rather solemn, as the whole school took their places in the big gym. Leslie had told everyone in his form that he was going to report the big boy, Robert, and some of the younger ones, who disliked Robert very much, had made up their minds that they too would tell about him if they had the chance.

'I should have told the truth about him when I was asked at the other Meeting,' said Peter. 'He did swing me much too high and made me sick – and afterwards he came to me and said he would open the door of my guinea-pigs' cage and let them escape, if I dared to say anything against him. So I didn't dare. But I wish I had now.'

William and Rita looked rather grave as they took their places at the table up on the platform. Rita had told William of the mean tricks that had been played on Jenny to get her into trouble, and the two Judges knew that they might have a rather difficult time trying to get at the bottom of things. Still, Miss Belle and Miss Best, and Mr Johns too, were at the back of the room. They could help if things got too difficult.

Robert looked pale. Elizabeth was red with excitement and so was Jenny. Joan was excited too, though she didn't show it.

The usual business was done with the box of money. The two pounds were given to everyone, and extra was allowed to two children for something they wanted. Then the Meeting got down to the real business of the evening.

'Any complaints or grumbles?' asked William, tapping on the table with his hammer.

Up jumped Elizabeth and Leslie, both together.

'Elizabeth was first,' said Rita. 'Sit down, Leslie. Your turn will come later.'

Leslie sat down. Elizabeth began to speak, her words almost tumbling over one another in her haste.

'William and Rita, I have a very serious complaint to make,' she said. 'It's the same one as Leslie was going to make. It's about Robert.'

'Go on,' said William, with a grave face.

'You will remember that I reported him for bullying Peter,' said Elizabeth. 'And because there wasn't enough proof of that, and because I lost my temper with Robert, the Meeting didn't punish Robert, and made me apologize to him. Well, listen to this!'

'Keep calm, Elizabeth,' said Rita. 'Don't get so excited.'

Elizabeth tried to speak calmly, but she did dislike Robert so much that it was difficult not to sound in a rage all the time.

'Well, William and Rita, Joan and I actually *saw* Robert bullying Leslie,' said Elizabeth. 'He made him sit on the hot-water pipes! And another thing we have found out is that he made Peter promise not to complain about being swung so high. He said he would let all Peter's guinea-pigs out of their cage if Peter dared to say anything against him at the Meeting. I was quite right – he is a horrid bully!'

'Don't call people names like that,' said Rita. 'Wait till the whole Meeting has judged, Elizabeth. Have you anything more to say?'

'Yes, I have,' said Elizabeth. 'And it's this: not only has Robert been unkind to the younger ones, but he has been perfectly horrid to me and Jenny too. He has got us into all kinds of trouble by playing mean tricks on us.'

'What tricks?' asked William, looking very worried.

'Well, he took three of my books and hid them somewhere where I can't find them,' said Elizabeth. 'He took my garden tools and dirtied them so that John scolded me. He put two of Jenny's white mice into Miss Ranger's desk and they escaped, and Jenny never found them!'

'Is that true, Jenny?' asked William.

Jenny stood up. 'It's quite true,' she said. 'I never found my poor little mice again. I don't mind a trick being played on *me*, William, but it's cruel to play it on my pets.'

'Sit down, Jenny,' said William. He spoke to Rita, and then turned to the School again.

'Leslie, stand up and say what you have to say,' he said.

The cheeky little Leslie stood up. He felt rather important. He put his hands in his pockets, and began rather cheekily: 'Well, it was like this . . .'

But William cut him short. 'Take your hands out of your pockets, stand up properly, and remember that this is a serious affair,' he said. Leslie took his hands out at once, and went red. He lost some of his cheeky look, and began to speak in a polite tone. He related exactly what had happened, and the Judges and Jury heard him patiently to the end.

'And now we should like to hear what Peter has to say,' said Rita. The small Peter got up. His knees were shaking again, for he was greatly in awe of the head boy and girl. He stammered as he spoke.

'P-p-please, William and Rita, Robert d-d-*did* swing me too high that time,' he said. 'And I was sick afterwards.'

'Then why did you tell an untruth about it when we asked you?' asked William.

'Because I was afraid to tell the truth,' said poor Peter. 'I was afraid of Robert.'

'You must never be a coward,' said William gently. 'It is much finer to be brave, Peter. If you had been brave and had told the truth, we could have stopped Robert from bullying others. Because you were afraid, you have been the cause of others being ill-treated, and you made us disbelieve Elizabeth, and made her unhappy. Remember to tell the truth always, no matter how hard it seems at the time. We shall all think much more of you if you do.'

'Yes, William,' said poor Peter, making up his mind that he would never be a coward again.

'You could have told your monitor about it, even if you were afraid to tell the Meeting,' said William. 'That is why we choose monitors – because we hope that their common sense will help us. Sit down, Peter.'

Peter sank down, glad that he hadn't to say any more. William looked at Robert, who was sitting looking sulky and unhappy.

'And now, Robert, what have you to say?' he asked. 'Serious complaints have been made against you. Are they true?'

'Only one complaint is true,' said Robert, standing up. He spoke in such a low voice that the Jury could not hear him.

'Speak up,' said William. 'What do you mean – only one complaint is true? Which complaint?'

'It is quite true that I made Leslie sit on the hot-water pipes,' said Robert, 'but anyway they weren't very hot. But I did NOT play any tricks on Elizabeth and Jenny. Not one! Not one!'

'Oooh!' said Elizabeth. 'You did, Robert! I saw how pleased you were each time I got into trouble!'

'Silence, Elizabeth!' said William. 'Robert, you say you did not play the tricks that Elizabeth described. Now you did not tell us the truth last time, when you told us about Peter and the swing. It will be difficult for us to believe you this time, because we shall all think that again you may be telling us untruths to get yourself out of trouble.'

'Well, I *am* telling the truth this time!' said Robert fiercely. 'I didn't play those tricks. I don't know who did – I jolly well know *I* didn't! I don't like Elizabeth, I think she's a horrid, interfering girl, but I'm not mean enough to play tricks like that to get her into trouble – and why should I play tricks on Jenny? I don't dislike Jenny. I tell you, somebody else is to blame for those tricks.'

Most unfortunately for Robert, there was not one person in the school, except Kathleen of course, who believed him. They all remembered that he had told an untruth before, and they felt certain that he was doing so again. William knocked on the table with his hammer, for the children had begun to whisper together.

'Silence!' he said. 'Now, we have a very serious matter to attend to. Three charges have been made against one boy. First, that he bullies smaller children than himself. Second, that he has played mean tricks to get two girls into trouble. Third, that he tells untruths. The Jury and Rita and I are going to discuss the matter to see what must be done about this, and the rest of you can also discuss it among yourselves, so that if anyone has a good idea, they may bring it forward in a few minutes.'

The school began to chatter. The Jury and the Judges talked together in low tones. They all looked extremely serious. Robert sat by himself, for the boys next to him had gone to talk to the children behind. He felt dreadful. Why, oh why had he been stupid enough to bully the younger ones? Why must he always be so unkind to the little ones? Now perhaps he would be sent home and his mother and father would be very angry and upset.

Miss Belle and Miss Best looked very serious too. Mr Johns said a few words to them, and then the three of them waited to see what the Judges would say. They never interfered with the school Meeting unless they were asked to.

After a little while Rita and William knocked on the table for silence. The whole school sat up. Surely the Judges and Jury hadn't decided so quickly! What were they going to say?

'Miss Belle, and Miss Best, and Mr Johns, we feel we would like your help today,' said William gravely. 'Would you please give us your advice?'

'Of course,' said Miss Best, and the three teachers came up on to the platform. And then began a strange talk that was going to make all the difference to Robert's school life!

13 Robert gets a chance

The whole school was now looking very solemn and serious. Not a smile was to be seen anywhere. Everyone stopped talking as the three teachers took their places on the platform, on chairs that the Jury quickly fetched for them.

'The matter had better be openly discussed,' said Miss Belle. 'Let us take one complaint at a time. First of all, this question of bullying the smaller ones. Now, have we ever had any cases of bullying since you became our Judges, William and Rita?'

'No,' said William. 'But I remember there was a case when I was much lower down in the school. Will it be in the Book?'

The Book was a record of all the complaints made by the children, and of how they had been dealt with, and what the results were. It lay on the table, a big brown volume half full of small writing. Each Judge had to enter in a report of the Meetings held, because Miss Belle and Miss

Best said that sometime the Book might be a great help. Now William took up the Book and began to look back through the pages.

At last he found what he wanted. 'Here it is,' he said. 'A girl called Lucy Ronald was accused of bullying younger children.'

'Yes, I remember,' said Miss Belle. 'We found out the cause of her bullying. Read it, William, and see what it was. It may help us with Robert.'

William read it quickly to himself. Then he looked up. 'It says here that it was found out that Lucy had been an only girl for seven years, and then she had twin baby brothers brought to live with her in her nursery,' he said. 'And her mother and father gave all their attention to them, and so did the nurse, so that Lucy felt left out. She hated the babies because she thought that her parents gave them the love they had always given to her.'

'Go on,' said Miss Belle.

'Well, she couldn't hurt the babies because they were never left alone,' said William. 'So she worked off her feelings of dislike and jealousy on other children – she always chose the smaller ones because they couldn't hit back, and because they were small like her baby brothers.'

'And I suppose the habit grew and grew until she couldn't stop it,' said Rita, interested. 'Is that how bullies are made, Miss Belle?'

'It's one of the commonest ways,' said the headmistress. 'But now, we must find out if Robert's fault is caused in the same way.'

The whole school had been listening with great interest to this discussion. Everybody knew what a bully was, and nobody liked bullies at all. The children looked at Robert to see if he was listening too. He was. He gazed at William, and didn't miss a word.

'Well,' said Mr Johns, 'we'll find out if Robert has anything to say now. Robert, have you any brothers or sisters?'

'I've two brothers, five years and four years younger than I am,' answered Robert.

'Did you like them when they were small?' asked William.

'No, I didn't,' said Robert. 'They took up everybody's time, and I didn't have a look in. Then I got ill, and nobody seemed to bother about me as they used to do, and I knew it was because of James and John, my little brothers. Well, when I got better, I just seemed to hate little children, and I began to pinch them and be unkind to them. I pretended they were James and John. I couldn't do it to them because nobody would let me, and I would have got into such a row.'

'And so a bully was made!' said Mr Johns. 'You made war on other children because you couldn't get rid of the two small brothers whom you thought took your place at home! Poor Robert! You make yourself much more unhappy than you make others.'

'Well, people have called me a bully ever since I was about five,' said Robert sullenly. 'So I thought I was one – something that couldn't be helped and that I couldn't stop!'

'Well, it can be helped, and you can stop it yourself,' said Miss Best. 'You see, Robert, once you understand how a bad habit began, and how it grows, you also understand how to tackle it. Now that we know why you became a bully, I am sure that none of us really blames you. It was just unlucky for you. You aren't really a bully – you are just an ordinary boy who took up bullying because you were jealous of two small brothers. You can stop any time, and change to something that is *really* you!'

'I remember being awfully jealous of my little sister,' said Belinda. 'I know how Robert felt.'

'So do I,' said Kenneth. 'It's a horrid feeling.'

'Well, it's quite a natural one,' said Miss Belle. 'Most of us grow out of it, but some don't. Robert just hasn't – but he will now that he sees clearly what has happened. It isn't anything very dreadful, Robert. But doesn't it seem rather silly to you that a boy of your age should be teasing and bullying Peter and Leslie just because years ago a feeling of jealousy grew up in your heart for your two young brothers? It's time you put all that behind you, don't you think so?'

'Yes, it is,' said Robert, feeling as if a light had suddenly been lit in the darkness of his mind. 'I'm *not* really a bully. I want to be kind to people and animals. I didn't know why I was the opposite – but now that I do know it will be easy to change. I feel different about it already. I'm sorry I was so beastly to other children all these years. But I'm afraid no one will trust me now – they won't help me!'

'Yes, we will, Robert,' said Rita earnestly. 'That is the great thing about Whyteleafe School – that we are all willing to help one another. There isn't a boy or girl in this school who would refuse to help you, or to give you a chance to show that you are quite different from what you have seemed.'

'What about Elizabeth?' said Robert at once.

'Well – we'll ask her,' said Rita. 'Elizabeth, what do *you* think about it?'

Elizabeth got up. Her mind was in a whirl. So Robert the bully wasn't really a bully – he was only a boy who had got a wrong idea about himself because of something that had happened years ago. It seemed very strange. Was it true? She didn't believe that Robert would change! And what about all those horrid tricks that had been played on her and on Jenny?

'Well—' said Elizabeth, and stopped. 'Well – of course I'll help if Robert wants to try. After all, you all helped me last term when I was dreadful. But I can't forgive him for playing those mean tricks on me and Jenny. I think he should be punished for those.'

'I tell you I didn't do them!' burst out Robert.

'Somebody must have done them,' said Rita. 'If Robert didn't do them, who was it? Is the boy or girl brave enough to own up?'

Nobody said a word. Kathleen went red but looked down at the floor. She had begun to feel rather dreadful now that Robert had been accused of her tricks.

'William and Rita, you didn't believe me before when I complained about Robert,' said Elizabeth. 'And I was right. It isn't fair of you not to believe me now. I'm sure I'm right.'

The Jury and Judges talked together. They found it very hard to decide anything. Then William spoke.

'Well, Elizabeth, you may be right. We did not believe you last time – and this time we will not believe Robert. We will try to make things fair between you by saying that you may play in the match tomorrow instead of Robert. Nora says that you were disappointed that you were not chosen.'

'Oh, thank you!' said Elizabeth, thrilled.

Robert stood up. He looked unhappy.

'Very well,' he said. 'I quite see that it's my turn to give way to Elizabeth this time, as she had to apologize to me last time when I told untruths. But I do say again and again that I didn't play those tricks.'

'We won't say any more about that,' said William. 'Now, Robert, we've been talking about how we can help you. Mr Johns says that the best thing we can do for you is to let you take care of something or somebody, so that it's easy for kindness to take the place of unkindness. You love horses, don't you?'

'Oh yes!' said Robert eagerly.

'Well, although your form are not allowed to have anything to do with the horses except ride them, we are going to make another rule just for you,' said William. 'You will choose two of the horses and make them your special care. You will feed them, water them, and groom them. When your class goes riding, you may choose one of the younger children to ride the second horse, and help him all you can.'

Robert listened as if he could not believe his ears. Good gracious! Choose two horses for his own special pets – look after them each day! This was a thing he had always longed to do, for of all animals the boy loved horses best – loved them with all his heart. He felt as if he could weep for joy. He didn't care about not playing in the match now! He didn't care about anything. He felt a different boy.

'Thank you *aw*fully, William,' said Robert in a rather choky voice. 'You can trust me to take care of the horses – and you can bet I'll choose those kids that I've teased, to take out riding first!'

'We thought you'd do that,' said Rita, pleased. 'Let us know at the next Meeting how you've got on, Robert. We shall all want to know.'

'I'll go riding with you, Robert!' called a small boy's voice. It was Peter. He had listened hard to everything that had been said, and in his generous heart he wanted to help Robert. He also felt a little guilty – for he remembered how once he had been jealous of his small sister and had smacked her when no one was looking. Good gracious, he might have turned into an unhappy bully like Robert!

'The Meeting must really break up now,' said Miss Belle. 'It has taken a long time and it is past the bedtime of the younger ones. But I think we all feel tonight that we have learnt something big – and once again you children have the chance of helping one of yourselves. It is grand to be helped – but it is even grander to help!'

'The Meeting is dismissed!' cried William, and knocked on the table with his hammer.

The children filed out, rather serious, but happy and satisfied. A difficult problem had been solved, and they were pleased.

Only one child was neither happy nor pleased. And that child, of course, was Kathleen! Robert had lost his place in the match because of her. Every child in the school was going to help him – but Kathleen had harmed him.

She was very miserable. But whatever could she do about it?

14 The day of the match

The next day was Saturday, the day of the lacrosse match. Elizabeth woke up early, and looked eagerly at the window. Was it a fine day?

It wasn't very fine. There were clouds across the sky. But at least it wasn't raining. Good! What fun it would be to play in her first match!

'Jenny!' whispered Elizabeth, as she heard the girl move in her bed. 'Jenny! It's the day of the match – and I'm playing instead of Robert!'

Jenny grunted. She wasn't sure if she was very pleased that Elizabeth should crow over Robert like that. Jenny thought Robert should certainly be punished – but crowing over him was another thing altogether.

Kathleen was awake too. She heard what Elizabeth said, and she felt guilty. She had thought that it was fine for another child to take the blame and the punishment for something she herself had done – but somehow she didn't feel like that now. Also, she was angry that Elizabeth should have the pleasure of playing in the match – for she did dislike Elizabeth so very much! What a nuisance everything was!

And what about Robert? Well, Robert also awoke early, and he remembered at once all that had happened the night before. He sat up in bed, his eyes shining, as he thought of the two horses he would choose for his own special care. He felt quite different. It didn't matter now a bit that the whole school knew he had been a bully – because they also knew it wasn't really his fault, and in a week or two he would be able to show them what he really was. What a surprise they would get!

He remembered the lacrosse match, and a little sinking feeling came into his heart as he remembered that Elizabeth was to take his place.

'I'd like to have played in the match,' he thought to himself. 'And it is jolly hard that the Meeting gave me that punishment for something I really didn't do – but I suppose they had to believe Elizabeth this time. I must put up with it and hope that the person who's really playing those tricks will be found out some time. Then everyone will be jolly sorry they punished me for nothing!'

He sat and thought for a while, his chin on his knees. 'Elizabeth is a funny girl. She's so fierce and downright, so keen on being fair and just – and yet she's been awfully unfair to me. She might know I wouldn't play mean tricks like that. I don't like her at all.'

Robert half made up his mind that he wouldn't speak to Elizabeth at all, or have anything to do with her. Then, as he thought of the lovely time he was going to have looking after the horses, his heart softened, and he couldn't feel hard even to Elizabeth! And anyway, he was going to show everyone that he could be kind just as easily as unkind.

'I know what I'll do!' he said to himself. 'I'll go and watch the match – and if Elizabeth shoots a goal I'll cheer like the rest. That will be a hard thing for me to do, but I'll do it just to show everyone I can!'

Robert got up before the others in his dormitory that morning. He slipped out and went to the stables. He would talk to the two horses he was going to care for – and he would go riding over the hills on his favourite. He felt proud and important as he unlocked the stable door and spoke to the stableman.

'Can I talk to Bessie and Captain?' he asked. 'I've got permission to look after them.'

'Yes, I've been told,' said the man. 'All right – but I'll have to oversee your work with them the first week, young man. After that, if you're all right, you can carry on.'

Robert heard running footsteps and looked out into the yard. He saw Leonard and Fanny hurrying to the cowsheds. They were going to milk the cows. They saw him and shouted:

'Hallo, Robert! Have you chosen your horses yet?'

'Rather!' said Robert. 'Come and see the two that are going to be mine! Look – this is old Bess – she's a darling. And this is Captain. Rub his nose.'

Leonard and Fanny looked at the two horses and then they looked at Robert. They stared at him so hard that Robert was puzzled.

'What's the matter?' he said. 'Have I got a smut on my nose, or something?'

'No,' said Fanny. 'But you do look different, Robert. You used to look so horrid – sort of sulky and mean – but now you're smiling and your eyes are all shiny. We're staring because it seems rather strange to see somebody change in a night! Come and see our cows! Would you like a glass of warm milk?'

The children linked their arms in Robert's and pulled him over to the cowsheds, where the patient cows stood waiting to be milked. They chattered and laughed as they went, and Robert felt warmed by their friendly talk and looks. He began to chatter too, and soon he was standing drinking a glass of warm, creamy milk from the first cow.

'This is fun!' he thought. 'I'll see Leonard and Fanny each morning when I come to see my horses. I shall soon make friends!'

In five minutes' time he was galloping over the hills by himself, enjoying the wind in his hair and the bump of the horse's back beneath him. He talked to Bess, and she pricked back her ears to listen. All horses loved Robert. He had never had a great deal to do with them before, and now it seemed to him almost too good to be true to think that he could have as much to do with them as he liked.

'After tea I'll ask young Peter if he'd like to come riding on Captain,' he planned. 'I'll soon make that kid forget all about the teasing I gave him.'

Everyone who met Robert that morning had a

grin for him, or a clap on the back. The whole school was keeping its word!

Neither Kathleen nor Elizabeth met him, for both girls were busy. Elizabeth was digging with John in the garden, and Kathleen had gone with some others for a Nature ramble. Elizabeth was chattering to John about the match.

'It's a bit of luck for me that I'm playing, isn't it?' she said. 'I was so disappointed when I saw Robert's name up on the board, instead of mine.'

'I expect Robert is feeling just as disappointed now,' said John, digging hard.

'Well, it serves him right,' said Elizabeth. 'He's been jolly mean to me and Jenny. Think how he dirtied my tools one night, John – and you blamed me for it.'

'I'm sorry I blamed you wrongly,' said John. 'I only hope you are right about Robert, Elizabeth, and that *he* is not being blamed for something he hasn't done either.'

'Well, he's a horrid boy, anyhow,' said Elizabeth. 'I'm glad he's out of the match. I bet he won't come anywhere near it. He'll be so ashamed that he's not playing after all!'

But that was just where Elizabeth was quite wrong!

The children playing the match had to change into their gym clothes immediately after lunch. The matches usually began at half-past two, so they hadn't a great deal of time. Kinellan School was arriving by bus at twenty-past two, and the Whyteleafe team had to be at the gate to meet them and welcome them.

Elizabeth could hardly eat any lunch, she was so excited. She stole a look at Robert, and saw that he was looking quite happy. Elizabeth pushed her potatoes to the side of her plate.

'Miss Ranger! I just can't eat any more. I'm so excited!'

'Well, for once you may leave what's on your plate,' said Miss Ranger, smiling. 'I know what it feels like to be playing in your very first match.'

Elizabeth rushed off with the others to change. Then she went to welcome the Kinellan team, and take them to the field. They put their clothes in the pavilion there.

'Look – almost the whole School has turned out to watch!' said Elizabeth to Nora, as she saw the children streaming up from the school.

'And there's Robert too!' said Nora, as she caught sight of Robert coming along with the others.

'Where?' asked Elizabeth in surprise. Then she saw him. Good gracious! Robert had come to watch the match he had hoped to play in! He had come to watch somebody play instead of him! The little girl could hardly believe her eyes. She suddenly felt rather small and ashamed. She knew she wouldn't have been able to do such a generous thing if she had been in Robert's place.

'I call it jolly decent of Robert to come and watch you play in his place,' said Nora. 'I think that's a big and generous thing to do. It's funny that a boy able to do a big thing like that should be mean enough to play horrid tricks. It makes me wonder if he really did do them, after all.'

Elizabeth picked up her lacrosse stick. She had felt so sure Robert wouldn't come near the match. She was quite wrong. And now suppose that, as Nora said, Robert hadn't done all the things she thought he had – suppose he was being punished unfairly? And all because of her! It wasn't a very nice feeling.

'Oh, well, never mind! I'm jolly well going to enjoy my first match!' said Elizabeth to herself, and she ran out of the pavilion into the field.

But what a disappointment – it was beginning to rain! The teams stared up into the sky in dismay. Surely the rain wasn't going to be much? Surely it would soon stop? It would be too bad if they couldn't play.

The children all crowded into the pavilion to wait. The rain fell more and more steadily. It pelted down. The clouds became lower and blacker – there really was no hope at all!

'I'm afraid the match is off,' said Mr Warlow. 'Go to the gym and we'll arrange games for the visiting team.'

The children ran helter-skelter to the school. Elizabeth ran too, sadly disappointed. It was too bad! Her very first match, and the rain had spoilt it!

A voice spoke in her ear. 'Elizabeth! Bad luck! I'm sorry!'

The girl turned – and saw that it was Robert who had spoken! He had run off to join the others, so she couldn't answer. Elizabeth stood still, astonished. *Robert!* Fancy *Robert* saying that! She simply couldn't understand it.

'Elizabeth! Do you want to be soaked to the skin?' cried Miss Ranger's voice. 'What are you doing standing out there like that? Come along at once, you silly child!'

And into the school with the others Elizabeth

went, very much puzzled, and not knowing quite what to do about it!

15 Kathleen owns up

Everybody was disappointed that the match was off, especially the players themselves.

The rain poured down all the afternoon. Mr Johns and Miss Ranger got some games going in the gym, and the visitors enjoyed themselves thoroughly.

Joan was sorry for Elizabeth's disappointment. She slipped her arm through her friend's. 'Elizabeth, never mind! There's another match next Saturday. Maybe you'll be able to play in that instead.'

'Perhaps,' said Elizabeth. 'But it really *is* bad luck that it rained today. I've been practising so hard, and really I'm getting quite good at catching the ball and shooting at goal!'

'I guess Robert was pleased that it rained so that you couldn't play,' said Joan.

'Well, Joan, that's the funny part – he was there to watch – and when it rained and we all went off the field, he came up and said it was bad luck

and he was sorry,' said Elizabeth. 'I really was
surprised. And somehow I felt rather mean.'

'Wait till he plays a few more tricks, then you
won't feel so mean!' said Joan.

But no more tricks were played. Kathleen
hadn't the heart to think of any more. She had
seen somebody else publicly punished for her own
wrong-doing, and she was beginning to despise
herself. She hated Jenny and Elizabeth, but it was
a miserable sort of feeling now, not a fierce red-
hot feeling.

'I'm a dreadful person!' thought Kathleen in
despair. 'I'm plain and spotty and pale. I'm dull
and slow, and now I'm mean and deceitful and
cowardly! That's the worst of beginning to do
horrid things – they make you feel horrid yourself,
and then you can't ever be happy any more. I'm
not fit to be at a school like Whyteleafe, where
the children are happy and jolly – and where
even a boy like Robert, who's been hateful to
others, can turn over a new leaf and begin again!'

Poor Kathleen! It had seemed such fun, and so
clever, at first, to think out nasty little tricks to
get Jenny and Elizabeth into trouble – but now
that she had found that mean ways make a mean
person, she hated herself.

'And it's much worse to hate yourself than it is to hate somebody else,' thought Kathleen. 'Because you can never get away from yourself. I wish I was a happy honest sort of person like Nora or John.'

Kathleen was really unhappy. She went about looking so miserable that the girls felt sorry for her.

'Don't you feel well?' asked Elizabeth.

'I'm all right,' said Kathleen, and walked off with her head drooping like a sad little dog.

'What's up, Kathleen? For goodness' sake, smile a bit!' cried Belinda. 'You're enough to turn the milk sour! Have you had bad news from home, or something?'

'No,' said Kathleen. 'I just don't feel like smiling, that's all. Leave me alone.'

Her work was so bad that Miss Ranger began to be worried. What in the world could be the matter with the girl? She looked as if she was worrying about something. Miss Ranger managed to get Kathleen alone for a few minutes, and spoke to her gently.

'Kathleen, my dear – is there anything wrong? Your work has gone to pieces this week, and you look so miserable. Can't you tell me what's wrong? I may be able to help.'

Kathleen felt the tears coming into her eyes when she heard Miss Ranger speaking to her so kindly. She turned her head away.

'Nobody can help,' she said in a funny muffled voice. 'Everything's gone wrong. And nothing and nobody can put it right.'

'My dear child, there are very few things that can't be put right, if only you will give somebody a chance to help,' said Miss Ranger. 'Come now, Kathleen – what's wrong?'

But Kathleen wouldn't tell her. She shook her head obstinately, and Miss Ranger gave it up. She could not like Kathleen, but she felt very sorry for her.

Then Kathleen made up her mind to do a very foolish thing. She would run away – right away home – but first she would tell Elizabeth and Jenny all she had done. She would confess to them, so that Robert would be cleared of blame. She could at least do that. She wouldn't despise herself quite so much if she owned up.

'Though it will be awfully difficult,' thought poor Kathleen. 'They will look at me in such a horrid way – they will call me names – and everyone in the school will know how awful I have been. But still, I shall have run away by then, so I shan't mind.'

That evening, after tea, Kathleen went up to Jenny. 'Jenny,' she said, 'I want to speak to you and Elizabeth alone. Where's Elizabeth?'

'She's in the gym,' said Jenny, surprised. 'We'll go and get her. What do you want, Kathleen?'

'I'll tell you when Elizabeth is with us,' said Kathleen. 'We'll go into one of the music practice-rooms. We'll be alone there.'

Very much puzzled, Jenny went with Kathleen to find Elizabeth. They soon found her and called her. Elizabeth went with them, surprised and rather impatient, because she had been having some fun with Belinda and Richard.

Kathleen closed the door and faced the other two. 'I've got something to say to you both,' she said. 'I've been very unhappy, and I can't bear it any more, so I'm going to go home. But before I go I want to own up to something. Don't blame Robert for all those tricks – *I* did them all!'

Elizabeth and Jenny stared at Kathleen as if they couldn't believe their ears. *Kathleen* had done all those things – hidden the books, taken

Jenny's mice, dirtied the garden tools, muddled the drawers? Oh, the horrid, horrid creature!

'I knew you would look at me like that,' said Kathleen, tears beginning to trickle down her cheeks. 'I expect I deserve it. But before I go, I'd like to tell you something else. You're both pretty and jolly clever, and everyone likes you. I'm plain and pale and spotty and dull, and I can't help it. But you don't know how I'd *like* to be like you! I envy you, and I can't help disliking you because you're all the things I'm not. You were very unkind once, Jenny, when you imitated Mam'zelle and me having a quarrel, but . . .'

'I'm sorry about that,' said Jenny at once. 'I didn't know you'd come into the room. I don't wonder you wanted to pay me out for that, Kathleen. But you shouldn't have got Elizabeth into trouble, too.'

'Well, I've paid myself out, too!' said Kathleen. 'I don't like myself any more than *you* like me. I know I'm simply horrid, and that's why I'm going home. My mother loves me, even though I'm not as pretty and nice as other girls are. And she will perhaps understand and forgive me for running away.'

There was a silence. Elizabeth and Jenny

simply did not know what to say. They were shocked at Kathleen's confession – and Elizabeth especially felt very angry because she had blamed Robert for things he hadn't done, and that was terrible.

'Well, Kathleen, all I can say is it's a jolly good thing you had the sense to own up,' said Jenny at last. 'I think more of you for that. But, my goodness, you're a spiteful mean person, I must say! Don't you think so, Elizabeth?'

'Yes, I do,' said Elizabeth. 'And you've made me get Robert into trouble – and I'll have all that to put right. I wish to goodness you'd never come to Whyteleafe School, Kathleen!'

'I wish it too,' said Kathleen in a low voice. 'But I shan't be here much longer!'

She opened the door and slipped away down the passage. She went to the stairs and ran up, tears pouring down her face. She had owned up – and it had been even worse than she had expected! Now she would get her things and go.

Elizabeth stared at Jenny, and the two were just going to talk about Kathleen's confession, when Joan came along. 'Hallo!' she said in surprise. 'What are you two doing here looking so fierce? What's happened?'

Elizabeth poured everything out to Joan. 'Now don't you think Kathleen is a spiteful girl?' she cried. 'I'd never have thought anyone could be so horrid.'

Joan looked thoughtful. She remembered how unhappy and lonely she herself had once been in the summer term, when everything had gone wrong. She could guess how Kathleen felt. And how very miserable she must be to think of running away!

'Look here,' said Joan, 'don't think of how mean and spiteful Kathleen's been. Think instead of how it must feel to be plain and jealous and dull, as Kathleen is, and to be unhappy and ashamed as well! Elizabeth, you were helped last term, and I was helped too. I'm going to help Kathleen! She hasn't been mean to me, so I don't feel angry about things as you do. I just feel sorry.'

She ran out of the room. Jenny looked at Elizabeth. They both knew at once that Joan was right. They had been thinking of themselves, and not of a miserable girl who needed comfort and help. 'We'd better go along too,' said Jenny.

'Wait till Joan's had time to say a few words,' said Elizabeth. 'She's awfully good at that sort of thing, you know. I sometimes think she's almost wise enough to be a monitor!'

'Well, we certainly are *not*,' said Jenny. 'I can't imagine how this can be put right, Elizabeth. I really can't.'

Meanwhile, Joan ran up the stairs to her dormitory. Kathleen was there, putting on her hat and coat, and packing a few things into a small case. Joan went straight up to her.

'Kathleen! I've heard all about it! You were brave to own up. Wait till Jenny and Elizabeth have had time to get over it, and they'll forgive you and be friends. They are kind and generous really, you know – just give them time.'

'I can't stop at Whyteleafe,' said Kathleen, putting on her scarf. 'It's not only that I've made enemies. I feel that everybody thinks I'm so awful. Look at your hair, all shiny and nice – mine's like rats' tails! Look at your bright eyes and red cheeks, and then look at me! I'm a sort of Cinderella!'

'Do you remember how Cinderella changed one night?' said Joan, taking Kathleen's hand. 'She sat in the cinders and moped, and maybe she looked just as plain and miserable as you do. But it wasn't just beautiful clothes and a coach that made her so different all of a sudden! Don't you think she smiled and looked happy, don't you think she brushed her hair till it shone? What a silly girl you are, Kathleen! Do you know that you look sweet when you smile?'

'I don't,' said Kathleen obstinately.

'Well, you do,' said Joan. 'Your eyes light up then, your mouth turns up, and you get a dimple in your left cheek. If you smiled a lot more, you wouldn't be plain long. Nobody's ugly when they smile. Haven't you noticed that, Kathleen?'

'Perhaps you are right about that,' said Kathleen, remembering how sweet her mother always looked when she smiled and was happy. 'But I never feel very much like smiling.'

Footsteps came up the passage and Elizabeth and Jenny came into the room. They went up to Kathleen.

'We weren't very nice to you just now,' said Jenny. 'We're sorry. Don't run away, Kathleen. We'll forgive you and forget all you did to us.'

'But Robert would have to be cleared from blame,' said Kathleen, 'and that means everything going before the school Meeting. I'm sorry – but I'm not brave enough for that!'

The girls looked at one another. Yes – of course

the matter would have to be discussed there!

'So I'm going!' said Kathleen. 'I'm a coward, I know. But I can't help that. Where's my case? Goodbye, all of you – don't think too unkindly of me, *please*!'

16 Kathleen runs away

Kathleen picked up her case and went out of the room. Joan ran after her and took hold of her arm.

'Kathleen! Don't be an idiot! You just can't run away from school! It's impossible!'

'It's not impossible,' said Kathleen. 'I'm doing it! Don't try to stop me, Joan. I'm going to walk down to the station to get the train.'

She shook off Joan's hand and ran down the passage. It wasn't a bit of good going after her. She had made up her mind, and nothing would stop her. The three girls stared at her.

'I feel simply awful about this,' said Jenny suddenly, in a trembling voice. 'I wish I hadn't imitated Mam'zelle and Kathleen that evening. That's what began all the trouble.'

'What are we going to do?' said Joan in a troubled voice. 'We'll have to report that Kathleen has run away. But I can't help feeling that it's no good trying to stop her in any way, because honestly *I* wouldn't want to face the school Meeting as she would have to do when everything comes out. She'd probably run away after that, if she didn't now! She's not a brave person at all.'

Just then Nora came by. She was surprised to see the three girls standing at the door of their dormitory, looking so worried.

'What are you here for?' she asked. 'Didn't you know that the concert is beginning in a minute? You'd better hurry. *Why* are you all looking so solemn? Has anything happened?'

'Well, yes,' said Elizabeth. 'An awful lot has happened. We don't know what to do about it. It's dreadful, Nora.'

'Good gracious! You'd better tell me about it then, as I'm your monitor,' said Nora.

'I think we'd like to,' said Jenny. 'Don't let's go to the concert, Nora. Let's go to the common room. It will be empty now and we can tell you what's happened.'

Once a week a concert was given by those children who learnt the piano, the violin, singing or reciting, and usually most of the forms attended, for it was fun to hear their own forms playing or singing. So the common room was empty when the four girls walked into it.

Jenny told the tale. She told it from the very beginning, and although she went red when she related how she had imitated Mam'zelle and Kathleen, she did not miss out anything. She was a truthful, honest girl, willing to take her fair share of any blame. Nora listened gravely.

'Poor old Kathleen!' she said. 'She *has* made a mess of things. Well, we've got to do something about it, but I daren't say what. We must find Rita and get her to come to Miss Belle and Miss Best with us.'

'Oh, goodness! Will they have to know?' asked Elizabeth in dismay.

'Of course, idiot! You don't suppose a girl can run away from Whyteleafe without the heads knowing, do you?' said Nora. 'Come on – there's no time to be lost.'

They found Rita in her study. 'Rita! Could you come with us to Miss Belle and Miss Best?' asked Nora. 'A girl in Elizabeth's form has run away, and we think we ought to tell the whole story to the heads.'

'Of course!' said Rita, looking startled. 'We'd better take William along too. It's a thing he probably ought to know about, and it will save time if he comes now.'

So in a few minutes six people were outside the drawing-room where the two headmistresses were sitting writing letters. Rita knocked.

'Come in,' said a quiet voice, and in they all went. Mr Johns was there too, and the three teachers looked surprised to see such a crowd of children appearing.

'Is anything the matter?' asked Miss Belle at once.

'There is, rather,' said Rita. 'Elizabeth, tell the story quickly.'

So Elizabeth told it all, and when she came to where Kathleen had packed a small case and gone down to the station, Mr Johns jumped up at once.

'I must go after her,' he said. 'I hope I shan't be too late.'

'But the train will have gone!' said Nora.

'They have been altered this month,' said Mr Johns. 'The one Kathleen went to catch doesn't run now – it's an hour later. If I go quickly, I can just get the child. Come with me, Rita.'

The two of them went out of the room, and in a moment or two the front door banged. They were gone. Elizabeth hoped and hoped that they would be able to catch poor Kathleen before she went home. Now that the heads knew everything she felt happier. Grown-ups always seemed to be able to put things right!

'Two things need to be put right, as far as I can see,' said Miss Best. 'The first thing is to put Kathleen right with herself, and make her see that running away never solves any difficulty at all, but only makes things worse. She thinks herself a failure, poor child, but no one need ever be that. If we can get that idea out of her head, things won't seem so bad to her.'

'And I know what the second thing is,' said Elizabeth in a low voice. 'It's to clear Robert of blame. I do hate to think I accused him unjustly – and he really has been decent about it. I feel terribly ashamed.'

'I am glad you feel ashamed, Elizabeth,' said Miss Best. 'We all know that you are just and honest by nature, but you will never do anything worthwhile if you rush at things impatiently and lose your temper.'

'No, I know. I'm doing my best to learn that,' said Elizabeth. 'But you've no idea how difficult it is, Miss Best.'

'Oh yes, I have!' said Miss Best. 'I once had a hot temper too!'

She smiled her lovely smile, and the four girls

thought what a nice person she was. None of them could really believe that she had ever had a bad temper.

'Now what are we going to do with Kathleen if Mr Johns is able to bring her back?' said Miss Belle. 'I almost think that William and Rita would be the best people to deal with her. She would not be so much in awe of them as she would be of me or of Miss Best or Mr Johns.'

'She said she couldn't possibly face the school Meeting when they knew of her mean tricks,' said Elizabeth. 'She isn't very brave – though sometimes she argues in class in a way I simply wouldn't dare to do.'

'That isn't bravery,' said Miss Belle. 'It's a thing that weak, obstinate people do – they are always so afraid of being thought poor things that they like to draw attention to themselves in some way – by arguing or quarrelling or boasting – anything that will make people listen to them and take notice of them! You will never find strong, wise people quarrelling or boasting or trying to get attention – only the weak ones. It's a sign of weakness of some sort – and in Kathleen's case it meant that she thought herself a failure and was trying to hide it from herself and from the rest of you. Now she can't hide it any more and she has run away – just what you would expect a weak person to do.'

'Things seem sort of different when they are properly explained, don't they?' said Jenny. 'I'd never have mimicked Kathleen as I did if I'd known why she was behaving like that. Now I feel so sorry for her that I'd do anything to get things put right.'

'She's ashamed of her spots, even,' said Elizabeth. 'She's only got them because she eats so many sweets! She eats more than the whole form put together!'

'She looks nice when she smiles,' said Joan. 'I told her so.'

'Good!' said Miss Best. 'It seems to me that if only Kathleen would make herself neater and prettier, and get rid of her spots, poor child, that would be a good beginning. William, do you think you and Rita can manage to get some sense into her head? You have had some difficult problems this term, but I believe you will manage them all right!'

'And what about making her face the school Meeting?' asked William.

'You and Rita must decide that,' said Miss Belle. 'We leave that in your hands. If you think it best not to force her to be brave before she is ready, then you must just clear Robert of blame, and wait until Kathleen is brave enough to own up later on in the term. I am quite sure that if we handle her gently she will do the right thing in the future.'

It was surprising how much better everyone felt already, now that the matter had been plainly discussed and looked into. Kathleen's bad behaviour had grown from a very simple thing – the feeling that she was a failure. If that feeling could be put right, most of Kathleen's troubles would go. And that would be pleasant for everyone!

There came the sound of wheels in the school drive. Then the sound of a car door banging. Surely it must be a taxi! Everybody waited anxiously to see if Mr Johns and Rita had been able to bring back Kathleen – and everyone hoped they had.

Footsteps came down the passage to the drawing-room and the door opened. Only Mr Johns stood there! No Rita, no Kathleen!

'Didn't you find her?' asked Miss Best anxiously.

'Oh yes!' said Mr Johns. 'She was in the waiting-room, poor child, cold and miserable, wishing that she hadn't run away after all! When Rita went in and took her hand, she burst into tears, and came back with us quite willingly. Thank goodness the trains had been altered, and she had had time to think a little. If the train had come in as soon as she had arrived on the platform, she would certainly have gone.'

'Where is she?' asked William.

'Rita has taken her to her study,' said Mr Johns. 'You go too, William. I think you'll be able to help her – let her talk all she likes, and get everything off her chest.'

William went. The four other children got up to go too.

'I'm going to find Robert now,' said Elizabeth. 'That's something *I* must put right – but I'm not going to enjoy it one bit!'

17 Clearing up a few troubles

Elizabeth was angry with herself as she went to find Robert. 'I've done a really awful thing,' she thought. 'I've accused somebody in public of doing a whole lot of mean things and he didn't do one of them. I got him punished – just at a time when he began to try and turn over a new leaf too! Everybody has helped him – and I was the only one who must have made him feel angry and unhappy. I do feel disgusted with myself.'

She couldn't find Robert anywhere. Then she met Leonard and he told her that the boy was out in the stables.

'Bess was limping a bit today,' said Leonard, 'and Robert is out there attending to her with the stableman. I saw him just now when I came in from the cowshed. You know, Elizabeth, Fanny and I see him every morning, and we think he's jolly nice. He's doing all he can to make up to the youngsters for ill-treating them – I can't help admiring him.'

'I admire him too,' said Elizabeth. 'But he won't admire *me* when he hears what I've got to tell him!'

'Why, what's that?' asked Leonard. But Elizabeth wouldn't tell him.

It was dark outside. Elizabeth got her coat and put it on. She slipped out into the garden and went across to the stables. She heard Robert talking to the stableman, and she put her head round the door.

'Robert,' she said, 'can I speak to you?'

'Who is it?' said Robert in surprise. 'Oh, you, Elizabeth. What do you want?'

He came over to her, smelling of horses. It was a nice smell. His hair was untidy and his face was flushed, for he had been rubbing the horse's leg with oil, and it was hard work.

'Robert,' said Elizabeth, 'I made a dreadful mistake about you. It was somebody else who played those tricks, not you.'

'Well, I told you that,' said Robert. 'That isn't any surprise to me.'

'Yes – but, Robert, I told the whole school you'd done them,' said Elizabeth, her voice beginning to tremble, 'and I got you punished. I can't tell you how sorry I am. You've been mean to me, often, and I haven't liked you, but I've been much meaner to you. And I do think you're a brick, the way you came to watch the match and told me it was bad luck it rained. I – I – I think you've been big, and I've been very small.'

'Well, I think you have, rather,' said Robert, taking her hand. 'But *I* haven't been very big, Elizabeth – it was only that I was so happy to think I've been able to change myself, and to have the horses I love, and I really felt I hardly cared about the match – so you see it wasn't very difficult to come and watch, and tell you it was bad luck it rained. But I'm glad you've found out it wasn't my fault that those tricks were played. Who did them?'

'I can't tell you just at present,' said Elizabeth. 'But as soon as I knew, I came to find you to tell you I was dreadfully sorry for what I'd said about you. I'd like you to forgive me.'

'You needn't worry about that,' said Robert, with a laugh. 'People have had to forgive me a lot more than I shall ever have to forgive *you*. Don't let's be silly any more. It's fun being enemies at first, but it soon gets horrid. Let's be friends. Come and ride Captain tomorrow morning before breakfast. I'll ride Bess if her leg is better.

And do cheer up – you look all funny!'

'I *feel* all funny,' said Elizabeth, swallowing a lump in her throat. 'I didn't think you'd be so awfully decent to me. I do get wrong ideas about people. Yes, Robert – I'd like to be friends. I'll be up early tomorrow morning.'

Robert smiled at her and went back to Bess. Elizabeth slipped away into the darkness. She stood in the cold wind and thought for a minute or two before she went in. How surprising people were! You thought some of them were so horrid, and believed all kinds of things about them – and then they turned out quite different and you wanted to be friends.

'Well, next time I'll give people a chance before I believe beastly things about them,' said Elizabeth to herself. 'I really must think twice, three times, *four* times before I lose my temper or accuse people of anything. It's so funny – I just hated Robert, and now I simply can't help liking him awfully – and yet he's the same person.'

But Robert wasn't quite the same person. He was different! He thought about Elizabeth too. It was brave of her to come and own up like that. She was a dreadful little spitfire, but he couldn't help liking her. It would be fun to ride with her and go galloping wildly over the hills in the early morning!

And meanwhile, what about Kathleen? Things had not been going too badly for her, for William and Rita had been wise and gentle, though quite firm and resolute. They had let the girl tell them every single thing.

'I felt awful when the train didn't come in,' said Kathleen, crying into her handkerchief, which was already soaking wet. 'I felt as if that was one more thing against me! I couldn't even run away because there wasn't a train!'

'It's a good thing you *couldn't* run away,' said William. 'It's not a very brave thing to do, is it? You can't get rid of troubles by running away from them, Kathleen. They go with you.'

'Well, what else can you do with troubles?' asked Kathleen, wiping her eyes.

'You can look them in the face and find out the best way to beat them,' said Rita. 'You were funny, Kathleen – you were really trying to run away from yourself! Nobody can ever do that!'

'Well, you'd want to, if you were like *me*,' said Kathleen. 'I'm so unlucky. Nothing nice ever happens to me, as it does to other children.'

'And nothing ever will as long as you think

and talk like that,' said William. 'It isn't our luck that makes good or bad things happen, Kathleen, it's just ourselves. For instance, you might say that Jenny has plenty of friends, so she is lucky. But she doesn't have friends because she is *lucky* – she has them because she is kind and generous and happy. It is her own self that brings her lots of friends, not her luck.'

'Yes – I see that,' said Kathleen. 'I hadn't thought of that before. But I'm not pretty and happy and generous like Jenny.'

'Well, why not make the best of yourself?' said Rita. 'You have a sweet smile, and you have a dimple that goes in and out, though we don't see it very often. If you brushed your hair one hundred times each night and morning as Jenny does, it would look silky and shiny. If you stopped eating so many sweets, your spots would go; and if only you'd go out for more walks and try to play games a bit harder, you would soon get rosy cheeks and happy eyes!'

'Should I?' said Kathleen, beginning to look more cheerful.

Rita fetched a mirror from the mantelpiece and put it in front of Kathleen's sad, tear-stained face. 'Smile!' she said. 'Go on, smile, you silly girl!

Quick! Let me see that dimple!'

Kathleen couldn't help smiling, and she saw her miserable face change in an instant to a much nicer one – and the dimple came in her left cheek.

'Yes,' she said, 'I do look much nicer. But I'm so dull and slow too – and think of the mean, horrid things I've done!'

'You're dull and slow because you're not as healthy as you might be, and you're not happy,' said William. 'Give yourself a chance, do! As for the mean, horrid things you've done – well, you can always make up for those. We all do mean things at times.'

'I'm quite sure you and Rita don't,' said Kathleen. 'And anyway, William and Rita – please, please don't make me stay at Whyteleafe, because I simply *couldn't* get up in front of the whole school at the next weekly Meeting and say what I'd done, even to clear Robert. I'm a coward. I know I am, so it's no good pretending that I'm not. I shall leave tomorrow morning if you make me do that.'

'We shan't make you do anything,' said William. 'It's no good *making* people do things like that! They must want to do them themselves, if it's to be any good. Well, listen, Kathleen –

we'll get Elizabeth to clear Robert of blame, but she shall not say who *is* to blame; but maybe later on you will feel differently about things, and then you can talk to us again.'

'I shall never be brave enough to own up in front of everyone,' said Kathleen. 'But I'll stay at Whyteleafe if I don't need to do that. I've told Elizabeth and Jenny and that was hard enough.'

'It was a good thing you did that,' said William. 'We will see that those children who know that it was you will not tell anyone else. So you need not be afraid that anyone is despising you. Do as Robert has done – turn over a new leaf – and smile as much as you can!'

'I'll try,' said Kathleen putting her wet hanky away. 'I don't *feel* like smiling. I don't even feel like turning over a new leaf. But you've both been so kind to me that I'll try, just to please you.'

'Good!' said Rita and William. Rita looked at her watch. 'It's almost your bedtime,' she said. 'Have you had any supper – or did you miss it?'

'I missed it,' said Kathleen. 'But I'm not hungry.'

'Well, William and I are going to make ourselves some cocoa,' said Rita. 'We are allowed to have our own gas-ring, you know, as we are the head children of the school. Stay and have some cocoa with us – and we've got some good chocolate biscuits too. Even if you are not hungry you will like those!'

In ten minutes' time the three of them were drinking hot cocoa and nibbling chocolate biscuits. William was making jokes, and Kathleen was smiling, her dimple showing in her left cheek. When her bedtime bell went, she got up.

'You *are* kind,' she said, tears coming into her eyes again. 'I won't forget this evening. I'm glad you're the head boy and girl – I think you're fine!'

'Cheer up!' said William. 'You'll find things are never so bad as they seem. Goodnight!'

18 Things are better!

Elizabeth was up early, and went out to the stables. Robert was there, saddling the horses, whistling softly to himself. He was completely happy. He was looking after something he loved, caring for the horses, and getting back from them the affection he gave them.

'It's a lovely warm feeling,' he told Elizabeth. 'I never had it before, because I never had a pet – and anyway, I never much cared for any animal except horses. William and Rita couldn't possibly have thought of anything nicer! It seems strange, doesn't it, that instead of being punished for bullying, I get a marvellous treat like this! And yet it's stopped me from being beastly far more quickly than any punishment would. I just don't want to be horrid now.'

'You can't be horrid to anyone when you're feeling happy,' said Elizabeth wisely. 'I know I can't. I just want to be warm and generous then. Come on – let's go. Oh, Robert, isn't it strange to be friends after being such dreadful enemies!'

Robert laughed as he sprang on to Bess's back. The horse whinnied and tossed her head. She loved to know that Robert was riding her. The two children cantered down the grassy path and then galloped off over the hills. Elizabeth had ridden for years, and rode well. Robert rode well too, and the pair of them enjoyed their gallop tremendously.

They shouted to one another as they rode. Then Elizabeth had an idea.

'I say!' she yelled. 'Will you take Kathleen Peters with you sometimes? She might get red cheeks then!'

'Kathleen! I can't bear her!' shouted back Robert. 'She's an awful girl. Surely you aren't going to be friends with *her*!'

'Well, I am,' cried Elizabeth. 'I don't like her, Robert, any more than I liked you. But I've been so wrong about people lately that for all I know I may get to like her very much. Anyway, I'm going to give her a chance. So will you help?'

'All right,' said Robert. 'She doesn't ride badly. But come too. I really don't think I could bear to go galloping with her by myself. I should be bored stiff! There's one thing about *you* –

nobody could ever be bored with you! You're either very, very nice, or very, very horrid!'

'Don't tease me about that,' said Elizabeth, slowing down her horse. 'I'm turning over a new leaf too! I want to be nice always. In fact, when I came back to Whyteleafe this term I had made up my mind to do my very, very best and be as nice as I could. And really, I've made the most awful muddles and mistakes! I know that I shall never be made a monitor!'

'You know, I'd rather like to be,' said Robert. 'It must be a lovely feeling to be trusted and looked up to, and to sit on the Jury's table. Still, we're neither of us ever likely to do that. I made a bad beginning this term – and you were the naughtiest girl in the school last term. My word, you *must* have been bad!'

Robert and Elizabeth were happy when they went in to breakfast that morning. Their cheeks were red with the cold wind, and their eyes sparkled. Elizabeth smiled at Kathleen, who was sitting in her usual place at the table, looking happier but rather nervous.

'Hallo, Kathleen!' said Elizabeth. 'Hallo, everybody! Gosh, I'm hungry! I could eat twenty sausages and twelve eggs!'

'Have you been riding?' asked Kathleen, pushing the toast towards Elizabeth. 'My goodness, you are red! The wind has made you look like a Red Indian!'

Elizabeth laughed. 'It was fun,' she said. 'You should get up early and come riding too.'

'Yes, do,' said Robert. 'You ride well, Kathleen. Why don't you come with Elizabeth and me sometimes? We could gallop for miles!'

Kathleen flushed with pleasure. She smiled warmly and everyone noticed at once how her dimple danced in and out. 'I'd love to,' she said. 'Thanks awfully. I like that horse called Bess best.'

'Do you really?' said Robert in surprise. 'How funny! So do I! She is a perfect darling, honestly she is. You know, she was limping yesterday and I was awfully worried.'

Soon he was telling Kathleen all about Bess and Captain, and Kathleen listened eagerly. She really knew quite a lot about horses, but for once she didn't boast, but listened humbly, glad that someone should speak to her in such a warm and friendly manner. She tried to remember not to let her mouth droop down at the corners in the way that made her so plain, but looked pleasant, and laughed at Robert's jokes.

She had been dreading that breakfast-time. It wasn't going to be easy to face Elizabeth, Jenny, Joan, and Nora, all of whom knew her poor, unhappy secrets. But after all it wasn't a bit difficult. Kathleen couldn't help feeling the warm generosity of the four girls near her, and it made her humble and happy instead of awkward and ashamed.

So breakfast was very pleasant, though some of the form were most astonished to see Robert and Elizabeth so friendly.

'You are a funny girl, Elizabeth,' said Kenneth. 'One day you are enemies and the next you are friends!'

'Last term Elizabeth was *my* bitterest enemy!' said Harry, with a laugh. 'I pinned a notice on her back, and on it was printed "I'm the Bold Bad Girl! I bark! I bite! Beware!" My goodness, how furious you were, Elizabeth!'

'Yes, I was,' said Elizabeth, remembering. 'But it seems rather a funny joke to me now. Let's go and look at the notice-board, Harry. I can see a new notice pinned up there.'

They went across to look at it. There *was* a new notice, rather an exciting one!

'Elizabeth Allen has been chosen to play in the

match against Uphill School,' it said.

Elizabeth stared at the notice, her cheeks on fire.

'Goodness!' she cried. 'I've *really* been chosen this time! Last time Robert was chosen, and I was to take his place – but this time *I've* been chosen! I *am* pleased!'

'Yes – and this time it's an Away Match, not a Home Match,' said Harry. 'You'll have the fun of going off in the motorcoach to Uphill School. You *are* lucky!'

'Oh, it's marvellous!' cried Elizabeth, and she danced away to tell Joan and Jenny. Kathleen was with them, and the four were all smiles as they discussed the match.

'If only we could come and watch you shoot a goal!' said Joan, slipping her arm through her friend's. 'I do hope it won't rain this time, Elizabeth.'

'Oh, it couldn't be so unkind!' cried Elizabeth. 'Joan! Kathleen! Come and give me some practice at catching before dinner this morning, will you!'

Kathleen beamed. So few children ever asked her to do anything. It was lovely to be wanted.

'You really *have* got a nice smile!' said Joan, looking at her. 'Come on – there's the bell. For goodness' sake hurry. I was half a second late yesterday morning and Miss Ranger nearly went up in flames about it!'

Kathleen found herself humming a tune as she ran to get her books. How decent the girls were! It was easy to smile when you were happy. Kathleen had smiled at herself once or twice in the mirror that morning, and really it was simply astonishing what a difference it made to her plain face! She had spoken sternly to herself.

'No more sweets for you! No more greediness! No more silliness at all! Smile and be nice, for goodness' sake!'

And the face in the mirror had smiled back at her, its dimple showing well. Who would have thought that a smile could have made so much difference to anyone?

When school was over that morning, Elizabeth rushed with Kathleen and Joan to get lacrosse sticks to practise catching and shooting. They bumped into Robert as they ran down the passage.

'Hey! What hurricanes!' said Robert. 'Whatever are you in such a hurry for?'

'We're going to give Elizabeth some practice at catching,' cried Joan. 'Didn't you know she has been chosen to play in the match against Uphill School on Saturday?'

'No – I didn't know,' cried Robert, his face falling for a moment, for he was bitterly disappointed. He had very much hoped that he would be chosen himself – for after all he *had* been chosen before, and Elizabeth had taken his place, though the match hadn't been played, as it happened. Now Elizabeth was chosen.

'Well, I mustn't be small about this,' he thought. 'I'll have plenty of chances to play in matches later on, I expect.' He shouted after Elizabeth:

'Good for you, Elizabeth! Wish I could watch you shoot a goal!'

He went off. Elizabeth turned to Joan. 'That was nice of Robert, wasn't it?' she said.

Joan looked at her. 'Did you see his face when he heard that you had been chosen?' she said.

'No, why?' asked Elizabeth in surprise.

'He looked awfully disappointed, that's all,' said Joan, getting out her lacrosse stick. 'I expect he hoped that he might get the chance this time, as he was prevented last time by the school Meeting.'

'Oh,' said Elizabeth. She got her lacrosse stick

too, and the three girls went out in the playing-field. Soon they were throwing the ball to one another, and then Kathleen went into goal and let the other two shoot the ball at her.

But Elizabeth didn't enjoy the practice very much after all. She was thinking of Robert. She had prevented him from being able to play in the match last Saturday – and she couldn't help feeling that it wasn't very fair that she should be playing *this* Saturday. 'Though, of course, I didn't play last Saturday because of the rain,' she said to herself. She caught the ball and threw it to Joan.

'But I *would* have played if it hadn't rained, and then I would have played two Saturdays running, and Robert wouldn't have played once – though he really was chosen last week. I'm beginning to feel uncomfortable about it. I think I'll go and ask Nora what she thinks.'

So after dinner Elizabeth went to find Nora. The monitors were always ready to hear anyone's troubles, and the children went to them readily.

'Nora! Do you think I ought to let Robert play in the match on Saturday instead of me?' asked Elizabeth. 'You know it was because of me that he was told he mustn't play last Saturday. Well –

I know he's disappointed about this. Shall I go to Eileen and tell her to let Robert play instead?'

'Yes,' said Nora at once. 'It's only fair, Elizabeth. Good for you! I'm glad you thought of that. There's one thing about you, you do like to be just, and that's a great thing!'

'I'll go and tell Eileen now,' said Elizabeth, and off she sped before she could change her mind. It was very disappointing for Elizabeth – but it would be a nice surprise for Robert!

19 A peaceful week

Eileen was in the gym. She was very good at gym and games of all kinds. She was busy doing some exercises, but she stopped when she saw that Elizabeth wanted to speak to her.

'What do you want, Elizabeth?' she asked.

'Eileen, would it be all right if Robert played in the match on Saturday instead of me?' asked Elizabeth. 'You see, I've discovered that he didn't do the things I accused him of at the last Meeting – so I think it would be only fair if I let him have the chance of playing this time.'

'Right!' said Eileen, taking out a notebook and writing something down in it. 'I'll see to that. As you say – it's only fair, Elizabeth. I'm sorry you can't play – but you've done the right thing!'

Elizabeth couldn't find Robert to tell him, and before she could do so, Eileen had taken down the first notice from the board and put up another.

'Robert Jones will play in the match against Uphill School on Saturday,' said the second notice.

Robert saw it as he came in to dinner. He stared at it in amazement. Surely Elizabeth had said *she* was playing! He stood frowning at the board, and Kenneth came up. 'Hallo!' said Kenneth, reading the notice. 'I wonder why that's altered. It said that Elizabeth was playing in the match, when I read it before breakfast!'

'Yes – that's what I thought,' said Robert, puzzled. 'Why has it been altered? But I say – that's marvellous for me! I was jolly disappointed this morning!'

'I bet Elizabeth will be disappointed too,' said Kenneth. They went in to their dinner. Robert did not like to say anything to Elizabeth in front of the others, and she said nothing about the notice either.

It was Nora who told Robert about it. 'Did you see that you were playing in the match after all?' she asked.

'Yes – but why?' asked Robert. 'What made Eileen change?'

'It was because Elizabeth asked her to let you play instead,' said Nora. 'Elizabeth thought that would only be fair. And I must say I agreed with her.'

Robert went red. 'It's awfully sporting of her,

but I can't let her do it,' he said. 'I know how badly she wants to play.' He went to find Elizabeth.

She was in the school garden, planting bulbs with John.

'Hi, Elizabeth!' called Robert. 'You're a sport – but I'd rather you played on Saturday, if you don't mind.'

'I shan't, Robert,' said Elizabeth. 'I've made up my mind. It's such a good way of trying to make up for the mistake I made. I should be ashamed of myself if I didn't do it.'

'But I don't mind whether you try to make up for your mistake or not,' said Robert.

'Yes, but *I* mind,' said Elizabeth. 'I shall think better of myself if I do this. Really I shall.'

'All right,' said Robert. 'Thanks. I only wish you were coming to watch, Elizabeth.'

'I hope you shoot lots of goals!' said Elizabeth, and went on with her planting. It was hard work. The crocus bulbs had come, and big patches of grass had to be lifted before the crocuses could be planted underneath. Then there were all the daffodil and tulip bulbs to plant too, though they were much easier to bury in the soil of the beds.

'There's so much to do and so little time to do

it all!' sighed Elizabeth. 'I would like to ride oftener – and I would like to garden all day long – and I'd like to have more music lessons – and I'd like to spend more time with the rabbits – and I'd like to play games oftener. I wish I was like you, John – and only had one favourite thing to do, instead of about twenty!'

'Well, I dare say you have a more exciting time than I have,' said John seriously. 'Mr Johns is always saying I ought to do something else besides gardening in my spare time, because I shall become dull.'

'I don't think you're a bit dull!' cried Elizabeth. 'I love to hear you talk about gardening!'

'Yes – because you like gardening and understand it,' said John. 'But to those who don't, I expect I do seem dull! You think of something else for me to do, Elizabeth.'

'Well, what about riding?' said Elizabeth. 'I never see you on horseback. Get Robert to take you out on Captain sometimes – he'd like that, and you'd enjoy it.'

The week went by, and Friday came. The school Meeting was to be held again that night. The children filed in as usual, not so grave as last time, for there were no serious matters to be discussed tonight. They always enjoyed the Meetings. They liked ruling themselves, making their own laws, and seeing that they were kept.

The extra money was put into the box. Kenneth proudly put in a whole ten pound note from one of his uncles. Peter put in five pounds. Then the week's pocket-money was given out.

John Terry asked for money for the new crocus bulbs and it was given him. He also asked for money for a new garden fork, a smaller one than the one he used.

'Peter is going to help with the digging,' he said, 'and our fork is too big for him. We've never had one suitable for the younger ones.'

That money was given out also. Richard asked for money to buy a record of a violin performance. He was anxious to play the same piece himself, and Mr Lewis had said that if he could get the record and hear how a great master played the piece it would help him. William granted the money at once. The whole School was becoming very proud of Richard, for he played both the piano and the violin beautifully. He sat down, pleased.

'Any complaints or grumbles?' asked William.

Leonard got up. He looked rather apologetic.

'This is rather a silly grumble,' he said. 'It's about Fred. He does snore so at night – and, you see, I have to get up early in the morning to milk the cows, so if I am kept awake by the snoring, I can't seem to make myself get up in time. We've all told Fred about it, but he can't help it. So what can we do?'

Fred stood up. 'I've had a bad cold,' he said. 'I think I'll be all right when it's quite gone. Shall I go and sleep in the Sanatorium by myself till Matron says I don't snore any more?'

'Yes, I should,' said William, smiling. 'It's about the funniest grumble we've ever had, I think. But Leonard *must* get his sleep or we shan't get our breakfast milk!'

Everyone laughed. William tapped on the table with his hammer.

'Before we dismiss,' he said, 'Elizabeth has something to say. Stand up, Elizabeth.'

Elizabeth stood up, red in the face. She had been thinking about what she had to say, and she said it straight out, without stammering or stopping.

'I want to say this,' she began. 'Last week I accused Robert of playing some mean tricks on me and on Jenny. You all believed me, and you said that Robert shouldn't play in the match as a punishment. Well, I was wrong. It wasn't Robert after all. It was somebody else.'

'Who was it? Tell us!' cried a dozen voices indignantly. William rapped on the table and everyone was quiet.

'Wait a minute, Elizabeth,' said William. '*I* want to say something. This is what I have to say: Rita and I, as Judges, have decided that for the present we shall not give you the name of the child who did the tricks. You know that in certain cases it is sometimes best not to refer the matter to the whole school. Well, this is one of them. I hope you will be satisfied that we are doing this for the best.'

'Of course!' cried half a dozen voices, for the head girl and boy were much liked and admired.

Poor Kathleen was sitting on her form with her knees shaking! She could not help thinking that the whole school must know it was she who had been so horrid. She looked down at the floor, and wished that a hole would come there so that she might go down into it and disappear! Jenny and Joan were sitting on each side of her, warm and comforting. They could feel Kathleen shaking and they were sorry. Well – it was a good thing that the Judges had decided to say no more about that!

Elizabeth was still standing up. She had a few more words to say. She waited for silence and then went on.

'I haven't got much more to say – except that I'm very sorry for what I said, and that in future I will always be careful to be quite sure before I accuse anybody. Robert was very nice about it indeed.'

She sat down. William was about to rap on the table to dismiss the Meeting, when Robert got up. He looked cheerful and bright, quite a different boy from the last Meeting!

'May I say something, William?' he asked. 'It's this. Elizabeth is letting me play in Saturday's match instead of her, to make up for saying wrong things about me. Well, I think that's very good of her, and I want the school to know about it!'

'Good old Elizabeth!' cried somebody. Everyone thought that Elizabeth had behaved justly and rightly. The girl could feel this, and she was happy.

Then the Meeting was dismissed, and the children filed out to do what they liked for the half-hour before supper.

Joan sat down to write to her mother. Jenny put on the gramophone and made up a dance in the middle of the floor, much to the amusement of the others. Elizabeth went to practise in one of the music-rooms. Robert began to read a book on horses.

Kathleen took up her sewing. She had spent all the money she had on two handkerchief-cases to embroider. One was to be for Jenny, and the other for Elizabeth. Rita had said that it was possible to make up for nasty things by doing something nice – so she was doing it!

'We learn a lot of things besides lessons at Whyteleafe School,' thought Kathleen, as she sewed. And she was right!

20 The great lacrosse match

Saturday came, marvellously bright and sunny. There was a frost in the morning, and the grass glittered white. But it disappeared in the sun, and everyone agreed that it was a perfect day for the match.

Elizabeth tried her very hardest to be glad that it was such a fine day. It was lucky for Robert; but she couldn't help feeling disappointed that she wasn't playing. She had missed playing the Saturday before because it rained and now that it was so fine, she couldn't play!

'Well,' she said to herself, 'it's your own fault, Elizabeth Allen; you shouldn't have been so foolish – then you would have been playing today!'

She went up to Robert when she saw him. 'I'm glad it's fine for you, Robert,' she said. Robert looked at her and knew what she was feeling.

'I wish you were playing too,' he said. 'Never mind – it will be your turn next time!'

The day kept fine. All the team who were going to play were in a great state of excitement. Nora was playing, and she told the others that Uphill School had never been beaten by Whyteleafe yet.

'If only we could beat them just this once!' she said. 'But I hear they've got an awfully good team. Eileen says they haven't lost a match yet this term. They really are frightfully good. All I hope is they let us get *one* goal!'

'Oh, Nora! We must get more than that!' cried Peter, a strong, wiry boy who was in the team. He was a marvellous runner and catcher. 'For goodness' sake let's put up a good show!'

'We'll do our best,' said Robert.

The morning went slowly by. Dinner-time came and the team could not eat very much, for they were all so excited. Elizabeth knew how she had felt the Saturday before. Oh, how she *did* wish she was going too! It was so terribly disappointing – but she was glad that she had been big enough to give up her place to Robert.

The sun shone in through the window. It was going to be a wonderful afternoon for a match. Elizabeth swallowed a lump in her throat. It was all very well to be big and brave and give up something because you thought it was right – but it didn't make the disappointment any less. Joan saw her face and squeezed her hand.

'Cheer up!' she said. So Elizabeth tried to cheer up and smile. And then she noticed something going on at the next table. People were getting up and talking – what was happening?

'It's Peter! He doesn't feel well,' said Joan. 'Isn't he white? I believe he's going to be sick. I didn't think he looked very well at breakfast this morning.'

Peter went out of the room, with Harry helping him. He did look very green. Mr Johns went out too. Mr Warlow looked at his watch. He hoped Peter would soon recover – because the coach was coming to fetch the team in twenty minutes.

Mr Johns came back in five minutes' time. He spoke to Mr Warlow, who looked disappointed. 'What's happened to Peter?' asked John, who was at the same table. 'Is he better?'

'He's got one of his tummy upsets,' said Mr Johns. 'Very bad luck. Matron is putting him to bed in the Sanatorium.'

'Golly!' said John. 'Won't he be able to play in the match then?'

'No,' said Mr Warlow. 'It's bad luck for our

team. Peter was one of the best. We must choose someone else.'

The news spread round the tables, and everyone was sorry about Peter. He really was such a good player. And then one by one the children called out something:

'Let Elizabeth play!'

'What about Elizabeth?'

'Can't Elizabeth play? She gave up her place to Robert!'

'Well,' said Mr Warlow, looking at his notebook, 'I had planned to get someone else next time – but as Elizabeth really deserves a trial, she shall play!'

Elizabeth's heart jumped for joy. She could hardly believe the good news. Her face went bright red and her eyes danced. She was sorry for Peter – but after all Peter had played in dozens of matches, and would again. Oh, she was really, really going to play after all!

'Good for you, Elizabeth!' called her friends, all pleased to see her shining face. The whole school knew, of course, that Elizabeth had given up her place in the match to Robert, and now they were really glad that she had her reward so unexpectedly.

Elizabeth sat happily in her place. Joan clapped her on the back, and Jenny grinned at her. 'Things always happen to you, don't they, Elizabeth?' said Jenny. 'Well, you deserve this piece of luck!'

'Elizabeth! I'm so glad!' called Robert from the end of the table. 'We shall be playing in our first match together! That'll be fun!'

Elizabeth couldn't eat anything more. She pushed her pudding-plate away. 'I shall feel sick, like Peter, if I eat any more,' she said.

'Well, for goodness' sake, don't then!' cried Nora. 'We can't have another player going sick at the very last moment!'

Elizabeth rushed off to change with the others into her gym things. She found time to peep into the San with a book for Peter. 'I'm sorry, Peter, old thing,' she said. 'I hope you'll soon be all right. I'll come and tell you about the match when it's over.'

'Play up!' said Peter, who still looked rather green. 'Shoot a few goals! Goodbye and good luck!'

Elizabeth shot off, her heart singing. It was too marvellous for words. Everyone laughed at her face and everyone was glad for her. She found Robert and took his arm.

'Sit next to me in the coach,' she said. 'We are the only ones who have never played in a match before – and oh, Robert, though I'm awfully happy, I feel a bit nervous!'

'*You* nervous!' said Robert, with a laugh. 'I can't believe it. A fierce person like you can't be nervous!'

But Elizabeth was! She was very anxious to do her best in the match, to do her best for Whyteleafe School. Suppose she played badly! Suppose she didn't catch the ball but kept dropping it! It would be dreadful.

'Still, there won't be anyone from Whyteleafe watching to see if I play badly,' she comforted herself. She looked at Robert as he sat beside her in the coach, looking burly and stolid and not a bit nervous. It was nice to be playing with him after all.

'I simply can't imagine how I hated him so much,' thought Elizabeth. 'It seems to me that if we dislike people, we see all the worst side of them because we make them show that to us – but if we like them, then they smile at us and show their best side. I really must try to give people a chance and begin by liking them, so that they show their best side at once.'

The coach soon arrived at Uphill School, which, as its name showed, was at the top of a steep hill. It was a much bigger school than Whyteleafe, and had the choice of far more children for its lacrosse team than Whyteleafe had. The Whyteleafe children looked at the opposing team and thought that they seemed very big and strong.

The teams lined up in their places. The whistle blew, and the game began. The Uphill team were certainly strong but there were some fine runners in the Whyteleafe team. They missed Peter, who was the finest runner of all – but both Robert and Elizabeth seemed to have wings on their feet that afternoon. They had never run so fast in their lives before!

Both children felt honoured to play in the match, and were determined to do their very best. Elizabeth's nervousness went as soon as the game began. She forgot all about herself and thought only of the match.

She and Robert often threw the ball to one another. Both children had practised their catching every day for some weeks, and were very good at it. Neither of them dropped the ball, but passed it beautifully.

'Good, Robert! Good, Elizabeth!' cried Mr Warlow, who was with the team. 'Keep it up! Shoot, Elizabeth!'

Elizabeth saw the goal not far off. She shot the ball at it with all her might. It flew straight at the goal – but the goalkeeper was on guard and shot the ball out again at once.

'Well tried, Elizabeth!' cried Mr Warlow.

Then the Uphill team got the ball and sped off towards the other goal, passing gracefully to one another – and then the captain shot hard. The ball rolled right into the goal, though Eileen, who was goalkeeper, did her best to stop it.

'One goal to Uphill!' said the umpire, and the whistle blew. The game began again, and both Robert and Elizabeth were determined not to let the Uphill team get the ball if they could help it.

Elizabeth got the ball in her lacrosse net and sped away with it. She was about to pass it to Robert, who was keeping near her, when another player ran straight at her. Elizabeth tripped over and fell. She was up again in a trice – but the ball had been taken by the Uphill girl. Down to the goal sped the girl, and passed the ball to someone else.

'Shoot!' yelled all the watching Uphill girls,

and the ball was shot towards the goal. It rolled inside before Eileen could throw it out.

'Two goals to Uphill!' called the umpire. He blew the whistle for half-time, and the girls and boys greedily sucked the half-lemons that were brought out to them. Oh, how lovely and sour they tasted!

'Now play up, Whyteleafe,' said Mr Warlow, coming out on to the field to talk to his team. 'Robert, keep near Elizabeth – and, Elizabeth, pass more quickly to Robert when you are attacked. You two are running like the wind today. Shoot at goal whenever there's a chance. Nora, feed Elizabeth with the ball when you can – she may perhaps be quick enough to outpace the Uphill girl marking her.'

The children listened eagerly. The Whyteleafe team were feeling a little down-hearted. Two goals to none!

The whistle blew. The match began again. Nora got the ball and passed it at once to Elizabeth, remembering what Mr Warlow had said. Robert kept near to her and caught it when she passed it to him. He passed it back again, and the girl sped towards the goal.

She flung the ball with all her might. The

goalkeeper put out her lacrosse net quickly – but the ball bounced off it and rolled into the goal.

'One goal to Whyteleafe!' said the umpire. 'Two to one.'

Elizabeth was thrilled. She couldn't keep still but danced up and down even when the ball was nowhere near her. Nora got the ball. She passed to Robert, Robert passed back, and Nora ran for goal. She shot – and once more the ball rolled right in! It was too good to be true!

'Two goals to Whyteleafe!' said the umpire. 'Two all, and ten minutes to play!'

The Uphill children, who were all watching the match eagerly, began to shout:

'Play up, Uphill! Shoot, Uphill! Go on, Uphill!'

And the Uphill team heard and played harder than ever. They got the ball – they raced for goal. They shot – and Eileen caught the ball neatly and threw it out again! Thank goodness for that!

Two goals all, and three minutes to play. Play up, Uphill! Play up, Whyteleafe! Three minutes left – only three minutes!

21 The end of the match

'Three minutes, Robert!' panted Elizabeth. 'For goodness' sake, let's play up. Oh, how I hope that Uphill School don't shoot another goal!'

The ball flew from one player to another. Elizabeth ran to tackle one of the Uphill girls, who was a very fast runner. She hit the girl's lacrosse stick and made the ball leap up into the air. Elizabeth tried to catch it but the ball fell to the ground. She picked it up in her lacrosse net, and tore off with it.

But another girl tackled her, and although Elizabeth tried to dodge, it was no use at all. She fell over and the ball flew into the air. The Uphill girl caught it neatly and raced off with it. She passed it to another Uphill girl who threw it vigorously down the field to the girl by the goal.

The girl caught it, and shot straight for goal. It looked as if the ball was flying straight for the goal-net – but Eileen saved it by flinging herself right out of goal! She fell over as she caught the ball, but somehow she managed to fling it to a waiting Whyteleafe boy. He caught it and was off up the field like the wind.

'Pass the ball, pass it!' yelled Elizabeth, dancing about. 'Look out! There's a girl behind you! PASS!'

The boy passed the ball just as the Uphill girl behind him tried to strike at his stick to get the ball. It flew straight through the air to Elizabeth. She caught it, and sped off, followed by a swift-running Uphill girl.

Elizabeth passed to Robert who was nearby. An Uphill girl ran at him – and he passed the ball back to Elizabeth, who ran for goal. Should she shoot from where she was? She might get a goal – and she would win the match for Whyteleafe!

But Robert had run down the field and was nearer the goal now – she ought really to pass to him! Without another moment's delay Elizabeth threw the ball straight to Robert.

He caught it – and flung it at the goal. It was a beautiful shot. The girl in goal tried her best to save the goal, but the ball flew past her stick and landed right in the corner of the net. Goal to Whyteleafe!

And almost at once the whistle blew for Time! The match was over!

'Three goals to Whyteleafe!' shouted the umpire. 'Three goals to two! Whyteleafe wins! Well played!'

Then all the watching Uphill girls cheered too, and clapped their hardest. It had been an excellent match and everyone had played well.

'Another second and the whistle would have blown for Time!' panted Elizabeth. 'Oh, Robert! You were marvellous to shoot the winning goal just in time!'

'Well, I couldn't have if you hadn't passed me the ball exactly when you did,' said Robert, his breath coming fast as he leaned on his lacrosse stick, his face flushed and wet. 'Well, Elizabeth – we've won! Think of that! We've never beaten Uphill before! Oh, I'm glad you shot a goal too!'

The two teams trooped off the field and went in to wash. It was nice to feel cold water, for they were all so hot! The two captains shook hands, and the Uphill girl clapped Eileen on the back.

'A jolly good match!' she said. 'It's the first we've lost this term. Good for you!'

Elizabeth hadn't been able to eat much dinner, but she made up for it at teatime. There was brown bread-and-butter and blackberry jam, currant buns and an enormous chocolate cake. The children ate hungrily, and the big plates of bread-and-butter and buns were soon emptied.

'I'm longing to get back to Whyteleafe to tell the good news,' said Robert to Elizabeth. 'Aren't you? Oh, Elizabeth, I *am* glad you played after all – and I can't tell you how glad I am that I was able to play! I hope we play in heaps more matches together. It was marvellous being able to pass the ball so well to one another!'

'You shot that winning goal well,' said Elizabeth happily. 'Oh, I'm so tired, but so happy. I feel as if I can't get up from this form! My legs won't work any more!'

All the children were tired, but their tongues still worked well. They chattered and laughed and joked together as they got ready to go back to the waiting motorcoach. Oh, what fun to tell the school that they had won!

They all got back into the coach. They waved goodbye to the cheering Uphill girls, and the coach rumbled off. The children sank back into their seats, their faces still red with all their running about, and their legs tired out.

But as soon as they got near Whyteleafe School

they all sat up straight and looked eagerly to see the first glimpse of the Whyteleafe children, who would all be waiting to hear the result of the match.

Joan and Jenny and Kathleen had been looking out for the coach for the last half-hour. When they heard it coming they tore to the big school door. Dozens of other children ran with them. It was always the custom at Whyteleafe to welcome home the children who had been to an Away Match.

The lacrosse team waved their hands wildly as the coach rumbled up to the big school door.

'We won! We won! Three goals to two!'

'We've won the match. It was marvellous!'

'It's the first time Uphill have been beaten!'

'Three goals to two! Three to two!'

The Whyteleafe children cheered madly when they heard the news. They swarmed out round the coach and helped down the team, whose legs were still very wobbly from all the rushing about they had done.

'Jolly good! Oh, jolly good!' cried everyone. 'Come along in and tell us all about it!'

So into the gym went the team, and Miss Belle and Miss Best, and Mr Johns too, had to come along and hear all the excitements of the afternoon. Mr Warlow spoke for a while and told how well everyone had played. Then John shouted out:

'Who shot the goals?'

'Elizabeth, Nora – and Robert,' said Mr Warlow. 'Good goals all three. Robert's was the most exciting because he shot his almost as the whistle went for Time. Another second and it would have been too late!'

'Three cheers for Nora, Elizabeth, and Robert!' cried everyone, and they clapped them on the back. How pleased and proud those three children were! Elizabeth almost cried for joy. To think she had actually shot a goal for Whyteleafe in her very first match. It was too good to be true.

Nora had played in many matches and shot many goals, so she just grinned and said nothing. But Robert was as pleased and proud as Elizabeth, though he did not show it quite so much.

Elizabeth slipped her arm in his. 'I'm *so* glad we both had the chance to play together,' she said. 'And oh, Robert, you don't know how pleased I am that I've done something for

Whyteleafe, even if it's only to shoot a goal! I hated Whyteleafe when I first came here – but now I love it. Wait till you have been here a term or two and you'll love it too.'

'I love it already, thank you,' said Robert. 'And what's more, I mean to do a whole lot more for it than just shoot a goal!'

There was a special supper that night for the winning team! Hot sausages appeared on the table, two for each one of the team. How delighted they were! And not only that, but anyone who had sweets or chocolates made a point of offering them to the team, so that by the time the bed-bell went, both Robert and Elizabeth felt that they couldn't eat anything more at all!

Kathleen was as delighted as anyone. Her face was beaming as she brought a tin of sweets along. Elizabeth took a good look at her.

'Golly, you don't look the same girl!' she said. 'Your eyes are all smiling and your hair is shiny! You walk as if you wanted to run, and you've already got rid of your awful spots!'

Kathleen laughed. She had kept her word to herself and hadn't eaten a single sweet. She had begun to forget herself, and to join in the chatter and jokes of the form. She held her head up and smiled gaily. Already when she thought of the horrid tricks she had played she could not imagine how she could have done them.

She had taken down Elizabeth's books from the top of the cupboard where she had put them, and had dusted them well. With scarlet cheeks she had given them back to Elizabeth, who had taken them with a word of thanks. A few scornful words had almost come to Elizabeth's tongue when she remembered how Miss Ranger had scolded her for losing her books – but she had bitten them back and said nothing.

Kathleen worked hard at the two handkerchief-cases, and embroidered them carefully and well. Each had the word HANDKERCHIEF across it, and it was a long word to sew. There were blue forget-me-nots on Elizabeth's case and pink roses on Jenny's.

Just as Kathleen was finishing the very last stitch, Jenny came into the common-room.

'My goodness, I wish I'd played in the match too,' she said, flinging herself into a chair. 'What wouldn't I do for hot sausages for supper! Hallo, Kath! What are you so busy about? Let's see.'

She bent over Kathleen's work. 'My goodness!' she said. 'What tiny stitches – and how nicely you've worked the roses! I wish I could sew like that. I want a handkerchief-case.'

'Well, this is for you,' said Kathleen, delighted. 'I've done one for Elizabeth too.'

'But whatever for?' asked Jenny, in surprise.

'To make up just a little bit for other things I did which weren't quite so nice,' said Kathleen. 'Here you are, Jenny – take yours and use it. I'm so glad to give it to you.'

Jenny was very pleased indeed. She took the handkerchief-case at once. 'You *are* a pal!' she said. 'Thanks a lot. Here's Elizabeth! Look – hi, Elizabeth, come and see what you've got for an unbirthday present!'

Soon both girls were examining their new handkerchief-cases in delight, and other children came round to see them. Kathleen felt proud when she heard their remarks.

'It's much nicer to do something *for* people instead of *against* them,' she thought. 'But I'll never, never be brave enough to own up to the School that it was I who played those tricks! I *am* nicer – and kinder too – but I'm still just as much a coward!'

22 Elizabeth in trouble again

The term went on happily. Now that the quarrels between Robert and Elizabeth, and between Kathleen and the others, had been cleared up, things were much better.

Elizabeth worked well and shot to the top of her class. Robert was sometimes second and sometimes third, which pleased Miss Ranger very much, for it was by sheer hard work that the boy did so well. Kathleen, too, worked a great deal better, and had stopped arguing in the silly way she once had. Mam'zelle was pleased with her.

'The child in this class who has made the most improvement is the little Kathleen!' said Mam'zelle. 'Ah, how I thought she was stupid! How I scolded her! But now, see, her French essay is the best, and she rolls her r's in the right French way – not like you, R-r-r-r-robert, who will never get them right!'

Robert smiled – and Kathleen went red with pleasure. She had never been praised in class before, and it was very pleasant. She began to wonder if she was as stupid as she had always thought herself to be.

'My memory does seem to be better,' she thought, 'and I like working at my lessons now. I was bored before. Maybe I shan't always be at the bottom of the class now! How marvellous! Wouldn't Mother be pleased if I came out top in something!'

She worked especially hard for Mam'zelle, and this was a great change for Kathleen, for ever since Mam'zelle had scolded her so badly she had disliked the French teacher and done her lessons carelessly. But now, somehow, things were different. For one thing the girl was healthier – she went out riding and walking with the others, and she even offered to help John, Elizabeth, and Peter in the school garden.

'Good gracious!' said John. 'You're the last person I would have thought wanted to help! Are you any good at gardening?'

'Well, no, not much,' said Kathleen honestly. Three weeks before she would have boasted untruthfully that she knew everything about gardening. 'But, John, I'd like to help a bit. Isn't there anything I can do?'

'You can wheel that rubbish over there to the rubbish heap,' said John. 'Then bring back the barrow and fork the next pile of rubbish in. It's really too heavy for Peter to wheel.'

Peter was very keen on gardening, and John was delighted to have him. Peter told John how Robert took him riding, and John grew quite interested in hearing about the horses.

'I'll really have to try riding myself,' he said. 'I've never much wanted to. I did when I first came to Whyteleafe, and then somehow I got so interested in gardening that I couldn't think of anything else. But perhaps I'll come tomorrow, Peter.'

Peter spoke to Robert, and it was arranged that John, Peter, Robert, Elizabeth, and Kathleen should all go riding together the next morning – and off they all went, galloping over the hills in the pale winter sunlight. John loved it.

'I must come again,' he said, when he jumped down from the saddle. 'That was fine. Goodness, Kathleen, what red cheeks you've got! You always used to look so pale! Coming to help me garden this weekend?'

'Yes, please,' said Kathleen, overjoyed at being asked to help someone. She was beginning to find how lovely it was to make friends, and to *be* a friend. If you offered to help other people, they offered to help you in return, and that was how friendships began – and surely it was the nicest thing in the world to have good friends round you!

'It was quite true what William and Rita said,' thought Kathleen to herself. 'I envied Jenny and said she was lucky because she had so many friends – and I thought that because I was an unlucky person none of those nice things happened to me. But now that I'm trying to be nicer, nice things happen to me too. It is our own selves that make us lucky or unlucky, it's our own selves that bring us friendship and kindness. I was always groaning and grumbling about everything and thinking I would always be unlucky and wouldn't be able to help it – but as soon as I changed myself, I changed the things that happened, too! What a pity that everyone doesn't know that!'

Elizabeth was working hard at her music, and Mr Lewis was very pleased with her. She and Richard were once again playing duets, and the big boy loved playing with the quick-fingered little girl. She looked up to Richard and thought he was wonderful.

'Can we play our duets at the school concert again?' asked Elizabeth. 'I do want to, Mr Lewis. Shall we be good enough?'

'Oh, yes,' said Mr Lewis. 'Richard is playing his violin, too. Have you heard him play the same piece that is on the gramophone record he got, Elizabeth?'

'No,' said Elizabeth. 'I haven't. But I'd like to. Please play it to me, Richard.'

So Richard was sent to fetch his violin, and the big, dreamy boy played a marvellous piece to his master and to Elizabeth. They both listened, enchanted.

'Oh, that's lovely,' sighed Elizabeth, when it was finished. 'Oh, I wish I could play like that. Can't I learn to play the violin too, Mr Lewis?'

'My dear child, you already fill your days too full!' laughed the music-master. 'No – stick to the piano.'

'But Richard plays the piano too,' said Elizabeth. '*And* the violin!'

'And he doesn't do anything else!' said Mr Lewis. 'But nobody can make him do anything else, so he might as well work hard at those. No one has ever made Richard pull a weed out of the garden, or ride a horse more than once, or keep even a harmless white mouse! He thinks of nothing but music.'

'I'll make him think of something else!' said Elizabeth. 'Come and practise with me at lacrosse tomorrow, Richard! You can't think how marvellous it feels to be good enough to play in a match!'

But Richard wouldn't come. He did play games sometimes, but so badly that he was worse than any child in the kindergarten. Not even determined little Elizabeth could make him leave his precious music, and she soon gave it up. Secretly she was very proud to play duets with him.

'One day Richard will be a famous musician and composer,' she told Jenny and Joan. 'Then I shall be very proud to think that once I played duets with him.'

There was to be a play at the school concert. The children in Elizabeth's form were to write one themselves, and they spent a long time thinking it out. When at last they had worked out the plot, there came the labour of writing it.

Jenny and Kathleen proved to be unexpectedly good at this. Jenny could manage conversation very well, and Kathleen had a good imagination and thought of all kinds of things. Before the week was out, the two were writing out the play together, with helpful and unhelpful remarks from the other members of the class.

It amused Elizabeth to see the two heads bent over the paper. 'It's just as funny to see Jenny and Kathleen like that as it was to see me and Robert,' she thought. 'How silly we are when we quarrel! Well – I'll never quarrel again!'

It was a pity she said that, for she broke her word to herself the very next day! She quarrelled with John!

They had built a big rubbish heap, and John had said they would light it the next time they had an hour or two to spare. But when Elizabeth went to find John in the garden to light the fire, he wasn't there.

'Oh, bother!' thought the little girl. 'I did so want to see the bonfire burning! Well – if John doesn't come in the next few minutes I'll light it myself. He won't mind.'

But she knew that he would mind, really, for although he trusted Elizabeth in a great many ways, things such as lighting bonfires he always did himself.

Elizabeth fetched a box of matches. She struck

one and held it to some paper she had pushed into the heart of the rubbish heap. It caught fire – and in a trice the bonfire was burning furiously! What a blaze it made! Blue smoke streamed out from it and flew over the shed nearby.

Elizabeth danced round happily. This was marvellous! How silly John was to be late!

And then she suddenly noticed something! The wind was blowing the flames of the bonfire near the shed!

'Oh! I hope the shed won't catch fire!' cried Elizabeth in alarm. 'Oh, my goodness – I believe it will! John! John! Quick, where are you?'

John was coming down the path at that moment. He saw the flames of the bonfire at the bottom of the garden, and hurried to see what was happening. When he saw that the red tongues were actually licking the woodshed, he had a terrible fright.

'Elizabeth! Get the hose out with me!' he cried. Together the two children unrolled the hose and hastily fitted it to the garden tap. John turned on the tap and the water gushed out of the hose. The boy turned it on the bonfire. In a few minutes the fire was out and only dense black smoke came from the very heart of it. John threw down the hose and turned off the tap.

'What in the world did you light the bonfire for?' he said angrily. 'What an idiot you are! Don't you know by now that I'm head of the school garden? You might have burnt down the shed!'

'Don't talk to me like that!' cried Elizabeth, firing up at once. 'You said *you* were going to light it – and it would have happened just the same if you had, wouldn't it?'

'My dear Elizabeth, I'm not *quite* so foolish as to light a bonfire just there, with the wind blowing the flames straight towards the shed,' said John furiously. 'Have a little sense! I didn't *dream* of lighting it today! And you've no business to. Now we've ruined the bonfire and I meant it to be such a beauty. You're a real nuisance, and I don't want you in the garden any more!'

'*Oh!*' cried Elizabeth, with tears in her eyes. 'You hateful boy! After all I've done in the garden and all the help I've given you!'

'You shouldn't have done it for me,' said John. 'You should have done it for the garden and for the school. Go away, Elizabeth. I don't feel I want to talk to you any more.'

'Well, I'll certainly never come and help in the garden again!' shouted Elizabeth, and off she marched in a great rage.

But half an hour later a little voice spoke inside her head. 'You said you weren't going to quarrel with anyone any more. And you have already! After all, John was right to be cross. You might have burnt down the shed and all his precious tools and everything – and you've spoilt the lovely bonfire he wanted to light.'

And a voice was speaking inside John's head too. 'Elizabeth didn't mean it. She was just silly, not bad. She's as disappointed as you are about the bonfire. And you know you *do* want her help in the garden. Suppose she takes you at your word and doesn't come any more? That wouldn't be very nice!'

'I'll go and find her,' thought John. And the same thought came to Elizabeth. 'I'll go and find John.'

So they met round the corner of the garden path, each looking rather ashamed. They held out their hands.

'Sorry I was piggy to you,' said John.

'And I'm sorry I was too,' said Elizabeth. 'Oh, John, I said to myself yesterday that I'd never quarrel with anyone any more – and I've gone and done it again!'

'You always will!' said John, with a laugh. 'But it won't matter if only you will make it up quickly. Come on and do some digging. It will do us both good.'

Off they went together, the best of friends. It takes more than a quarrel to break up a real friendship, doesn't it?

23 A *thrill* for Joan

Two months of the Christmas term had already gone by. Seven school Meetings had been held, and the eighth was to be held on the next Friday night. A new monitor had to be chosen, because one of the old ones, a boy called George, had the flu, and was in the San for a week or two.

'How are new monitors chosen?' asked Robert. 'Nobody new has been chosen since I came at the beginning of the term. I thought monitors were only chosen for a month – but we've had the same ones for two months.'

'Yes, because they're so good we don't want to change them,' said Joan. 'We *can* change them at the end of each month if we want to – but there's no point in changing them if we are satisfied. I think all our monitors are awfully good.'

'So do I,' said Elizabeth. 'I once thought it must be awful to be a monitor and have to keep all the rules and see that the others did too – but now I've changed my mind. I think it's rather nice to be trusted so much, and to have people coming to you for help and advice.'

'Well, the people who matter in this world are the ones who can be really trusted and who are willing to help anyone in trouble,' said Jenny. 'We get good training for that at Whyteleafe! One day *I'd* like to be a monitor – but like you, Elizabeth, I know I never shall be!'

'Well, nobody's answered my question yet,' said Robert patiently.

'What *was* it?' asked Elizabeth.

'I asked how new monitors are chosen,' said Robert. 'Do we choose them – or do the Jury – or the Judges – or who?'

'Well, the whole school chooses them first,' said John. 'We each write down the name of one we think we would like as monitor, and then the slips of paper are folded and passed up to the Jury.'

'What next?' asked Robert.

'The Jury undo them and see which three children have the most votes,' said John. 'They vote for whichever of those three they think would be best. Then their votes are passed up to William and Rita – and the two Judges decide which child is to be made a new monitor.'

'I see,' said Robert. 'It seems very fair. Everyone has a say in the matter. That's what I like so much about Whyteleafe – we all have a say in things.'

'I can't quite think who to vote for,' said Jenny. 'I'll have to think hard.'

'So will I,' said Joan thoughtfully. 'It is such an honour to be chosen. The one we choose must really be worthy of it.'

'Can I walk with you when we go for our Nature ramble this afternoon?' asked Kathleen. 'Elizabeth can't go – she's got an extra music practice with Richard.'

'All right,' said Joan. 'But don't be late. I'm leading the ramble, you know, and you must be on time if you want to start off with me.'

Kathleen was very punctual, and the two set off together with their notebooks, followed by the rest of the children who were interested in Nature work. They were to find blossoming ivy, the last insect feast of the season, and to list and draw all the insects feasting on the nectar in the green blossoms.

It was fun to wander down the lanes together and over the fields. The pale winter sun shone down and the sky was the faint blue of a harebell.

The trees were all bare except the firs and the pines, and the frost still glittered under the hedges.

Kathleen hummed a little song to herself as she looked about for the blossoms of the ivy. Joan looked at her.

'It's funny how people change,' she said. 'Last term I saw Elizabeth change from a horrid, naughty girl to a kind and good one. I felt myself change from somebody lonely and shy to somebody quite different. I've seen Robert change – and now you're changing too under my very eyes!'

'Yes, I know,' said Kathleen. 'But there's one way I haven't changed, Joan. I'm still a coward!'

'How do you mean?' asked Joan, surprised. 'Are you frightened of cows, or something?'

'No, of course not,' said Kathleen. 'I'm frightened of what people think! That's much worse than cows! Nobody but you and Jenny and Nora and Elizabeth know that it was I who played those horrid tricks – oh, and Rita and William, of course. And I know quite well that if it had been you or Jenny or Elizabeth you would all have been brave enough to get up in front of the whole school at a Meeting and say it was you!'

'Well, of course,' said Joan. 'Why not? You know quite well that the school would think well of you for owning up, and not so badly of you for doing the tricks. But if it leaks out that you *did* do them and didn't own up, why then, we should think much worse of you, and you'd think worse of yourself too! It's just a question of making up your mind to do it. Everybody has plenty of courage – only they don't always use it.'

'Have they really?' asked Kathleen. 'I mean, have I got plenty of courage if I like to use it? I don't *have* to be a coward then?'

'You *are* an idiot!' said Joan, taking Kathleen's arm. 'I mean what I say. No one has to be a coward – anyone can draw on their courage the moment they make up their mind to! Try it at the next Meeting – you'll see what I mean then.'

They found a great stretch of blossoming ivy just then, so they said no more, but busied themselves in writing down the large list of insects hovering over the nectar. But Kathleen was thinking over Joan's words. It would be too marvellous if they were true. If everybody had courage deep down inside them, why then, nobody need be a coward – they only had to take hold of their courage and use it!

'I'll see if I can use mine at the next Meeting,' thought Kathleen, though her heart sank at the thought. 'It's tiresome to see all the other children standing up and saying things, and I hardly dare to open my mouth!'

So at the next Meeting, unknown to any of her friends, Kathleen sat with shaking knees, trying to take hold of her courage. The usual business was gone through – money put into the box – money given out – money granted or refused for several things. And then came the complaints and grumbles.

There was only one complaint and only one grumble, and they were quickly dealt with. Then, before the other business of choosing a monitor was put before the Meeting, William said a few words.

'I think the school would like to know that Fred is back in his dormitory, and doesn't snore any more.'

There was laughter at this, and a few cheers. Fred laughed too. William knocked on the table.

'I also want to say this – that the whole School has noticed and approved of the way that Robert has behaved for the last few weeks. Rita and I have had excellent reports from all the monitors. Also the stableman says that he really couldn't do without Robert now to help him with the horses.'

Robert flushed with pleasure. The school was pleased too – it was always good to hear that they had been right in their treatment of anyone.

And then Kathleen found her courage, took hold of it with two hands and stood up. Her knees no longer shook. Her voice was steady. She looked straight at the Judges and the Jury.

'I want to say something I should have said before,' she said. 'I want to say that I was the person who did all the things that Robert was accused of. I was afraid to own up before.'

There was complete silence. Everyone was most astonished. Those who hadn't known were surprised to hear the news – and those who had known were even more surprised to hear Kathleen owning up! Whatever had made her do it so suddenly?

Then Rita spoke. 'And what has made you able to own up now?' she asked.

'Well, it was really something Joan said,'

explained Kathleen. 'She told me there was no need for *any*one to be a coward. She said we all had courage in us, only we had to take hold of it. So I took hold of mine this evening – and Joan was right. I wasn't afraid any more.'

'Thank you, Kathleen,' said Rita.

Kathleen sat down. Her heart was light. She had got rid of a heavy load. She had found her courage – and she wasn't going to lose it again!

'We won't say any more about what Kathleen has confessed to us,' said Rita. 'We are all glad she has been brave enough to own up. William and I knew it was she, of course – and we hoped that one day she would be able to tell you herself. Now she has – and we are pleased.'

'We had better get on with the business of choosing a new monitor,' said William. 'Give out slips of paper, please, Eileen.'

The slips were given out. Everyone wrote down the name of a girl or boy they thought fit to be a monitor. The papers were given to the Jury and opened. The Jury then chose out the three names that had most votes and voted on them themselves. Their papers were given to the two Judges.

William and Rita opened the twelve slips of

paper from the Jury. They talked to one another in low voices whilst everyone waited eagerly to know who had been chosen.

Then William knocked on the table with his hammer, and everyone was perfectly quiet. 'There isn't much doubt as to who you want for a new monitor,' he said. 'Her name appears on almost everyone's paper. It is Joan Townsend!'

There were cheers and clappings, and Joan went as red as a beetroot. She had had no idea at all that the school would choose her! But everyone had heard with interest what Kathleen had said about Joan's wise word on courage – and now Joan's reward had come! She was to be the new monitor.

'We have had excellent reports of you from all the other monitors,' said Rita. 'We know that you are to be trusted, that you are kind and wise for your age, and that you will do your best for the whole school. Please come up and sit at the monitors' table, Joan – we are glad to welcome you on our Jury!'

Joan went up to the platform, proud and happy. Elizabeth clapped madly – she was so proud of Joan, so pleased that she was honoured in this way.

'Joan deserves it!' she thought. 'She really does! My goodness, if only I could be a monitor too! But I'm not the right sort of girl, and never will be!'

24 A horrid adventure

The term slipped into December. The school was very busy planning and preparing plays and songs of all kinds. The weather was unkind, and many afternoons there were no games to be played out-of-doors.

'It's even too bad to garden,' groaned John, looking out of the window. 'The ground is so sticky that I can't dig.'

'Anyway, you'd get soaked through,' said Joan. 'It's a good chance for you to take an interest in something else! But I expect you'll get down one of your gardening books and pore over that!'

Joan was very happy to be a monitor. She took a great pride in her new honour, and did her duties well. She had to see that the children in her care did not break the rules of the school. She had to advise them when they came to her for help. She had to act wisely and kindly always – and this was not difficult for her because she was naturally a sensible and kindly child.

Elizabeth was very pleased that Joan was a monitor. She did not feel jealous, of course, but she longed to be one too. Still, Joan had been at Whyteleafe for far longer than Elizabeth – so she must wait her turn in patience. Though patience was not a thing that Elizabeth possessed very much of at present!

Elizabeth practised her music pieces hard and played the duets over and over again with Richard, for she was very anxious to do her best at the concert. Mr Lewis praised her.

'Elizabeth, you are working very hard. You are playing extremely well this term.'

Elizabeth felt proud. My goodness! She would show everyone at the concert how well she played! If her father and mother came to the concert they would be surprised to see Elizabeth playing such difficult duets with a big boy like Richard!

'You're getting conceited about your playing, Elizabeth,' said Richard one afternoon. Richard never thought twice about what he said, and he could be very hurtful. 'It's a pity. I like your playing – but I shan't like *you* if you get conceited.'

'Don't be so horrid, Richard,' said Elizabeth

indignantly. 'I don't tell you *you're* conceited, do I!'

'No, because I'm not,' said Richard. 'I know quite well that my gift for music is nothing to do with *me* really – it's something that has been given to me – a real gift. I'm thankful for it and grateful for it and I'm going to use it for all I'm worth – but I'm not conceited about it and never shall be.'

Elizabeth was annoyed with Richard – especially as she knew that what he said was just a little bit true. She *was* getting conceited about her playing!

'But why shouldn't I be proud of it?' she thought. 'I haven't got a wonderful gift for it like Richard – so my playing is my own hard work, and I've every right to be proud of that!'

So she went on planning to show off at the school concert, and make everyone think what a wonderful pianist she was. But pride always comes before a fall – and poor Elizabeth was going to have a dreadful shock.

She and Robert, John and Kathleen, had arranged to go out riding one afternoon before games. Peter came running up and begged Robert to let him go too.

'No, you can't, Peter,' said Robert. 'The horse you usually ride is limping – and I don't want you to have the other. It's a restive horse. Wait till your horse is all right.'

'Oh, please, do let me ride the other horse,' begged Peter. 'You know I'm a good rider!'

'Let him come, Robert,' said Elizabeth. 'You know he can ride Tinker.'

'Well, but Tinker really *is* a bit funny today,' said Robert. 'I'll see what he's like when two o'clock comes, Peter.'

When two o'clock came, Robert was not in the stables. The others were there. Elizabeth saddled the horses and looked for Robert. Still he didn't come.

'Oh bother!' said Elizabeth. 'It's ten-past two already. Wherever has Robert got to? We are wasting all our time.'

Peter sped off to look for Robert – but he came back in a few minutes to say that he couldn't find him.

'Well, if we're going for a ride we'd better go!' said Elizabeth. She called to the stableman.

'Hi, Tucker! Can I saddle Tinker? Is he all right?'

'Well, he's a bit upset about something,' said

Tucker. 'You have a look at him, Miss.'

Elizabeth went to Tinker's stall. The horse, which was a small one, nuzzled into her hand. She stroked his long nose. 'He seems all right,' she said. 'I'll saddle him for you, Peter. I'm sure Robert would say you could ride him.'

She saddled him quickly. Peter leapt up on to his back, and the four children cantered out into the paddock. Then away they went down the grassy field path, the girls' hair streaming out in the wind.

'We shan't have time to go very far,' shouted Elizabeth. 'We've only got about twenty minutes. We'll go as far as Windy Hill and back!'

They cantered out into a lane leading to the hill. And then something happened!

As they trotted round a corner, a steam-roller started rumbling down the lane, which had just been mended. Tinker reared up in fright, and Peter held on with all his might.

Elizabeth cantered up beside him and put out her hand to hold the reins tightly – but the horse tossed its head, gave a loud whinny, and darted into an open gateway that led to a field.

And then it ran away! The three children stared in fright. Poor Peter! There he was on Tinker, holding on for dear life, whilst the horse galloped like mad across the stony field towards Windy Hill.

'I'm going after him!' cried Elizabeth. She swung her horse round and galloped through the gateway. She shouted to him, and smacked him on his broad back. He set off swiftly, knowing that he had to overtake the runaway horse.

Over the stony field went Elizabeth, whilst John and Kathleen watched in fright. Far away galloped Tinker, Peter still clinging fast.

Elizabeth's horse was bigger and faster than Peter's. He galloped eagerly, his heels kicking up the stones. Elizabeth urged him on, shouting loudly. It was a good thing that she was such a good rider and that she trusted her horse! On and on they went, gaining little by little on Tinker.

Peter's horse was panting painfully. He began to climb the steep Windy Hill and dropped to a trot. Peter tugged at the reins and tried to bring him to a stop, but the horse was still terribly frightened.

Elizabeth galloped her horse up Windy Hill and at last overtook Tinker. But Tinker started in fright as soon as the other horse came up beside him. He stretched out his neck and began to gallop off again.

But Elizabeth had managed to get the reins, and when Tinker felt her strong little hand on them, he quietened down, and listened to her voice. Elizabeth was good with horses and knew how to speak to them. After the first tug to get rid of Elizabeth's hand, Tinker slowed down and then, trembling from head to foot, stopped still.

Peter was trembling too. He climbed down at once. Elizabeth leapt down and went round to Tinker's head. In a few minutes she had quieted the horse, but she did not dare to ride him.

'Peter, ride my horse and go back and join the others,' she said. 'I shall have to walk Tinker home. Tell the stableman what has happened, and take a message to Mr Warlow for me to tell him I shan't be back in time for games. Go on, now!'

Peter rode back to the others on Elizabeth's horse. He soon recovered himself, and began to boast about the runaway horse. The three children rode home and gave Elizabeth's message – whilst poor Elizabeth had to walk Tinker home for a very long way.

The little girl was tired and upset. Something

dreadful might have happened – Peter might have fallen from the horse and been badly hurt! Why had she let him ride Tinker without first getting Robert to say he could? Well, it was Robert's fault for being late for the gallop!

Her left hand hurt her. She had got hold of Tinker's reins with it when she had tried to stop him, and somehow her wrist had been twisted. She tucked it into her coat, hoping it would soon be better. She was very miserable as she walked back over the fields and lanes, leading a tired and steaming horse.

The stableman was not pleased. Robert came running out when he saw Elizabeth coming back, and he was not pleased either.

'Elizabeth! I've heard all about it! How *could* you be so silly as to let Peter ride Tinker! I couldn't help being late. Mr Johns kept me to do something for him. You might have waited! This wouldn't have happened then, for I would never have let Peter ride Tinker in that state. You are always so impatient and cocksure of yourself!'

Elizabeth was tired and her hand was hurting her. She burst into tears.

'That's right! Be a baby now!' said Robert in disgust. 'I suppose you think that if you cry I'll be sorry for you and not say any more! That's just like a girl! It's a good thing for you that neither Tinker nor Peter have come to any harm!'

'Oh, Robert, don't be so unkind to me,' sobbed Elizabeth. 'I've hurt my hand, and I can't tell you how badly I feel about letting Peter ride Tinker.'

'Let's have a look at your hand,' said Robert, more kindly. He took a look at the swollen wrist. 'You'd better go right away to Matron. That looks pretty bad to me. Cheer up! It's no good crying over spilt milk!'

'I'm not!' said Elizabeth, wiping her eyes. 'I'm crying over a runaway horse and a hurt wrist!' And off she went to find Matron, nursing her hurt hand. Poor Elizabeth! Things always happened to her.

25 Elizabeth is very tiresome

Elizabeth went to find Matron. She was in the Sanatorium with two ill children there. She came out when Elizabeth knocked at the door.

'What is it?' she asked. 'You can't go in!'

'I know,' said Elizabeth. 'I've twisted my wrist and I thought perhaps you could do something for it.'

Matron looked at the swollen wrist. 'That must hurt you quite a lot,' she said. 'How did you do it?'

Elizabeth told her. Matron soaked a bandage in cold water and wrapped it tightly round the hurt wrist.

'Will it soon be better?' asked Elizabeth. 'It's a good thing it's not my right hand.'

'It will take a little time to get right,' said Matron. 'Now, keep it as still as possible, please. And look – I will make you a sling out of this old hanky – like that – round your shoulder. That will help a bit.'

It was past teatime by now. Matron took Elizabeth into her own room and made some toast. Elizabeth was tired and pale, and although she said she didn't want anything to eat, she couldn't help thinking that the buttered toast looked rather nice. So she soon ate it up and drank the cocoa that Matron put before her.

Then she went off to the common room. Everyone was waiting to hear what had happened. Joan ran to her at once.

'Elizabeth! Is your hand badly hurt?'

'Well, it hurts a bit now,' said Elizabeth, 'but it's not nearly as bad as it was, since Matron bandaged it. It's all my own fault, as usual! I was impatient because Robert was late and I saddled Tinker for Peter – and Tinker ran away.'

'Poor old Elizabeth!' said Jenny.

Robert said nothing. He sat reading a book. He still looked cross.

There came a knock at the common room door and small Peter poked his head in. 'Is Elizabeth here?' he asked. 'Oh, there you are, Elizabeth. I say – how's the wrist? I'm awfully sorry about it. I suppose you won't be able to play the piano for a little while now.'

Elizabeth hadn't thought of that for one

moment. She stared in dismay at Peter. 'Oh, my goodness!' she said. 'I had forgotten that. Oh *dear* – and I so badly wanted to practise hard this week, and now I've only got one hand!'

Everyone was sorry for her. Robert raised his head and looked solemn. 'Bad luck, Elizabeth!' he said. 'I hope your hand will be well enough to play at the concert.'

Elizabeth was upset. She felt the tears coming into her eyes and she got up quickly. She hated people to see her crying. She went out of the room and went into one of the little music-rooms. She sat down at the piano and leaned her head against the music-rack. She was angry with herself for doing something silly that had ended, as usual, in bringing trouble on herself.

Richard came along humming. He didn't see Elizabeth at the piano, and switched on the light to practise. He was surprised to find her in the dark, all alone.

'What's the matter?' he asked. 'What are you crying for?'

'Because what you said has come true,' said Elizabeth sadly. 'You told me I was getting conceited about my playing – and that pride comes before a fall. Well, you were right. I did something silly, and now I've hurt my wrist and I can't play the piano, so I don't expect I'll be able to play duets with you at the concert.'

'Oh, I *am* sorry!' said Richard, in dismay. 'Now I suppose I'll have to play them with Harry, and he's not nearly so good as you. Oh, Elizabeth – what bad luck for you!'

'You shouldn't have said pride comes before a fall!' wept Elizabeth. 'I feel as if you made this happen!'

'Oh, don't be so silly,' said Richard. 'No, really, that *is* silly, Elizabeth. Anyway, cheer up – it may not be as bad as you think. I'll play to you, if you like. Get up and let me come on the stool.'

Elizabeth got up. She went to the chair in the corner and sat down, tired and cross. She didn't like Richard. She didn't like Robert. She didn't like Peter and his runaway horse. She didn't like herself. She didn't like anybody at all! She was a cross, unhappy, tired girl who didn't want to be pleased with anything or anybody!

But Richard's music made things much better. The little girl's frown went away and she leaned back feeling happier as the soft notes of the piano fell into the silence of the little room. Richard knew exactly what music to play to comfort her.

She stole away in the middle of his playing and went back to the common room. Perhaps her wrist would be better by the next day. Perhaps she was making a fuss after all. The others looked up as she came in.

'Come and do this puzzle with me,' said Kathleen. 'I can't find the bits that go just here.'

Everyone was kind to her, and Elizabeth was grateful. But she was glad when bedtime came, for her legs ached and her wrist still hurt her. Matron had a look at it and bound it up again.

'Keep it in the sling,' she said. 'It won't hurt so much then.'

Elizabeth hoped it would be better when she awoke in the morning. But it was still swollen and tender, though it did not hurt quite so much. She couldn't possibly play the piano with it! It was too bad!

And then Elizabeth found how difficult it is to do even the most ordinary things with one hand instead of two! She couldn't tie her hair-ribbon! She couldn't tie her shoelaces! She couldn't wash herself properly. She couldn't do up a button. She couldn't even seem to blow her nose easily.

The others did what they could for her, but Elizabeth was not easy to do things for. She wouldn't stand still – she jerked her head about when Joan tried to do her hair. She stamped her foot when poor Kathleen tried her best to do up the buttons of her blouse and got them all wrong.

'Oh dear – you've gone back to being the little girl who had a little curl right down the middle of her forehead!' sighed Joan. 'And you're being very, very horrid!'

'Well, so would you be if this had happened to you!' said Elizabeth, in a rage. 'If it had been my right hand I could at least have missed all the exams next week – but as it is I'll be able to do the exams, and have to miss the things I really love, like gym and riding and music! Oh, it's just too bad!'

In a few days' time Matron said Elizabeth could use her hand again – but alas for Elizabeth, she seemed to have no strength in the hurt wrist, and did not dare to use it much. The doctor said she must do what she could with it, and that gradually it would be all right – but she must be patient.

Well, that was just the one thing that Elizabeth couldn't be. She was upset and she showed it. She was annoyed and everyone knew it. She was furious because Richard was now practising the duets with Harry. And when she found that she couldn't be in the play because her part, which was that of a soldier, meant doing some drilling and exercising with a wooden gun, which her wrist couldn't manage – well, that was just the last straw!

The form were worried about Elizabeth, and disappointed in her. They talked about it.

'She's just getting crosser and crosser,' said Jenny. 'Nobody can do anything with her. She can't help thinking about herself and the nice things she's missing all the time. It *is* bad luck that she can't even play games. She does love them so.'

'Let's think of some things for her to do,' said Joan sensibly. 'There's George in the San, getting better. Couldn't Elizabeth go and read to him? Then there's all the programmes to make out for our play. Elizabeth is awfully good at designing things like that. Let's ask her to help us. She can easily do it with her right hand. And there's those gold crowns we have got to make – Robert says he'll make them – and surely Elizabeth could paint them with gold paint?'

Everyone agreed that it would be a good thing to get Elizabeth to do a few things so that she might forget her crossness. So one by one they went to her and asked her for her help.

Now Elizabeth was sharp, and she soon guessed why the children were suddenly asking her to do things for them. At first she felt that she would refuse – why should she do things for them when she couldn't do anything nice for herself at all? Joan saw her face, and took hold of her arm.

'Come along with me,' she said. 'Let's have a talk, Elizabeth. I'm a monitor now and I have a right to tell you a few things and to help you.'

Elizabeth went with her into the garden. 'I know all you're going to say,' she said. 'I know I'm behaving badly. I'll never be a monitor like you. I'll never be able to forget myself and not mind when things go wrong.'

'You're a goose, Elizabeth,' said Joan patiently. 'You don't know what you can do till you try. There are only two weeks left of the term. Don't make them miserable for yourself. We all like you and admire you – don't let a little thing like a hurt wrist spoil our liking and admiration for you. You really are being rather trying. Everyone has been as kind and patient as possible. You make things very hard for your friends.'

Elizabeth kicked a stone along the path. After

all, why should she make things horrid for her friends when her hurt wrist was her own fault and nobody else's? It *was* rather feeble of her. She took Joan's arm.

'All right, Monitor!' she said. 'I'll help you all I can. I'll do the programmes – and read to George – and paint the gold crowns. If I can't be a sport for two weeks I'm not much good!'

'It's just because you're such a strong person really that we don't like to see you suddenly being awfully weak,' said Joan. 'All right – now do your best for us, Elizabeth!'

Once Elizabeth had really made up her mind to do something she could always do it. She could be just as patient as she could be impatient. She could be just as cheerful as she could be cross. And in the very next hour her friends saw the difference!

She set to work on the programmes. She could manage to hold the paper with her left hand, and it was quite easy then to draw and paint with her right. Soon she had done half a dozen excellent programmes and the whole form came to admire them. Elizabeth was pleased.

'Now I'm going to be a good girl and go and read to George,' she said, smiling cheerfully round. And off she went, leaving the others laughing.

'She can be a monkey but you can't help liking her!' said Jenny. And everyone agreed!

26 A marvellous surprise

The last week of the term came. Exams were held every day, and the children worked hard. Elizabeth, Robert, and Kathleen worked the hardest of all, for each of them wanted to do well. Elizabeth longed to be top of her form, and so did Robert. Kathleen wanted to be top in *something*, she didn't mind *what*!

'It would be so lovely to tell Mother I was top in something,' thought Kathleen. 'I'm always so near the bottom – and Mother has been so perfectly sweet about it. It really would be a marvellous surprise for her if I could do well in something.'

Elizabeth's wrist was much better, but she still could not use it for playing the piano, and neither was she allowed to go riding, to play games, to dig in the garden, or to do gym! It really was very hard luck indeed.

She was in the songs at the concert, but not in anything else. She was not in the play and she was not playing with Richard. Harry was taking her place.

She tried to be cheerful, and she did not let anyone see how miserable she sometimes felt. She had pulled herself together, and was doing all she could to help the others in every way. She had painted the crowns marvellously for the play, and had even painted some trees for the scenery. Everyone thought they were wonderful.

She had done twelve programmes, the best that had been done in the school. Miss Belle was to have one and so were Miss Best and Mr Johns. Elizabeth was proud of that.

She had been to read to George and to play games with him every day till he had come out of the San. She had done lots of little jobs for Matron. She couldn't help John in the garden as she had been used to doing, but she wrote out lists of flower seeds for him, ready for the spring, and listened eagerly when he told her all he and Peter had been doing.

'She's really being a brick!' said Joan. 'There's good stuff in our Elizabeth! She can be the naughtiest girl in the school – but she can be the best girl too!'

Elizabeth went to watch the hockey and

lacrosse matches, and cheered the players, though deep down in her heart she felt very sad because she too was not playing. It was awful not to be able to do any of the things she liked so much.

'You know how to grin and bear things, Elizabeth,' said Richard. 'I'll say that for you!'

Nothing that Elizabeth had ever done made the school admire her as much as they did the last weeks of the term. Everyone knew what a fiery, quick-tempered child she was, and they knew how hard it must be for her to be cheerful, patient, and helpful. They were proud of her.

The school concert came. It was a most exciting afternoon. All the parents who could come, came to hear it. Mr and Mrs Allen were there, and were going to stay at a hotel the next day so that they might take Elizabeth back with them. Elizabeth flew to meet them, and they hugged her in delight. They were sad to hear that her hurt wrist prevented her from taking any real part in the concert, but they loved the programme she presented to them.

'I did it for you,' said Elizabeth proudly. 'Do you like it? The heads have my programmes too. And Mummy, please notice the gold crowns in the play, because I painted them – and the trees too.'

The concert was a great success. The play was funny and made the audience laugh loudly. Jenny and Kathleen were thrilled, because it was they who had written it out for their form. Richard played the violin most beautifully, and he and Harry played the duets that Elizabeth had been going to play.

She felt sad when she heard them, but she made her face smile all the time, and clapped hard at the end. She saw Jenny, Joan, Robert, and Kathleen watching her, and she knew that they were proud of her for being able to smile and clap, when inside she was very disappointed.

At the end of the concert the results of the exams were given. Elizabeth listened with a beating heart. So did Robert and Kathleen. Jenny did not care much – so long as she was somewhere near the top, that was all she minded! Kathleen cared much more. She knew she had done her best, and she hoped she wouldn't be too near the bottom!

At last Miss Belle came to Elizabeth's form. 'Miss Ranger says that this form has done exceedingly good work,' she said. 'Some of the children have been surprisingly good. First comes Elizabeth Allen and . . .'

But Miss Belle couldn't go on, because a storm of clapping interrupted her. Everyone seemed to be delighted that Elizabeth was top! Robert clapped hard too. How he hoped that he might be second! He had half hoped he might be top – but never mind, he might be second!

Miss Belle held up her hand for silence. 'Wait a moment,' she said. 'Let me finish what I had to say. First come Elizabeth Allen *and* Robert Jones! They have tied for first place, so they are both top.'

Robert sat up straight, his face bright with surprise and delight. So he and Elizabeth were top together! That was almost better than being top by himself. Elizabeth was sitting just behind him and she bent forward and clapped him on the back.

'Robert,' she said, her face beaming, 'I'm *awfully* pleased! I'd rather be top with you than top by myself, honestly I would!'

Robert nodded and smiled. He couldn't speak because he was so pleased. He had not such good brains as Elizabeth, so he had had to work really hard to win his place – and how proud his father and mother looked!

Miss Belle read down the list. Jenny was fourth. Joan was fifth, and both girls were pleased. Kathleen was sixth, well away from the bottom – and she had top marks in history! Her cheeks glowed as she heard Miss Belle read that out. She was fairly near the top – and she had the best marks in history. What would her mother say to that? Kathleen stole a look round the big gym, and saw her mother's face. One look at it satisfied Kathleen. Her mother was looking as happy as anyone in the room.

'I can't think what Whyteleafe has done to my little Kathleen,' her mother was thinking. 'She looks quite different. She was always such a plain child, poor little thing, but now she's really pretty when she smiles – and how happy and bright she looks with all her friends!'

It was a splendid afternoon – and in the evening the last school Meeting was to be held. There was a surprise for the school then, which William did not announce until after the usual business had been dealt with.

All the money was emptied out of the box and evenly divided between each girl and boy. This was always done at the end of term, and the children were pleased, because it meant that they started their holidays with a little money in their pockets.

Then William made his announcement. 'I am sorry to say that we are going to lose Kenneth this term,' he said. 'Kenneth's father and mother are going abroad and he is to go with them. So we shall not see him again until they come back, which will not be for six months.'

The school listened in silence. 'I should like to say that we thank Kenneth very much for being a wise and good monitor for many terms,' said William. 'He has done many kind and generous things that most of us know nothing about, and we shall miss him very much. We shall be very glad when you come back, Kenneth.'

'Thank you,' said Kenneth, going scarlet. He was a quiet, shy boy, liked by everyone. The School was sorry to say goodbye.

'Well, as Kenneth will not be here to be a monitor next term, we have to choose another new one,' said William. 'You may like to have George back again, of course, or you may like to give someone else a chance if you think there is anyone worthy of being tried as a monitor. Nora, give out slips of paper, please.'

Nora rose, and gave out the slips of paper to

each boy and girl. They took them and sat, thinking hard. It was unexpected to have to choose a monitor without talking about it between themselves first. Elizabeth chewed her pencil. Whom should she put? She decided on John – though she half felt that John wouldn't be a *very* good monitor, because he only understood one thing really well, and that was gardening! Still, it might be good to give him a chance. So she wrote down his name – John Terry.

Soon everyone had written down a name. The papers were given to the Jury, who unfolded them and counted them. Then the Jury, too, considered the matter and at last handed in their own papers.

William and Rita undid them, said a few words to one another, and then William knocked on the table with his hammer.

'Three names have been given the most votes,' he said. 'One is John Terry – the second is Robert Jones, whom the younger ones have voted for (you should be pleased about that, Robert!) – and the third is – Elizabeth Allen.'

Elizabeth jumped. She had no idea at all that anyone would vote for her – or would even *think* her good enough to be a monitor. She had the surprise of her life!

'Now we have heard a great deal of Elizabeth this term,' said William. 'Some good, and some bad. But both Rita and I have noticed how well Elizabeth has tackled a big disappointment these last few weeks – and has tried to forget herself and to help her form in every way. So it is no wonder that so many people have voted for her.'

'We know that she brought disappointment on herself,' said Rita, 'but we mustn't forget that she hurt her wrist in trying to stop Peter's horse. It was a brave thing to do. Elizabeth, you are a real mixture! You can be foolish and you can be wise. You can be impatient and you can be patient. You can be unkind and you can be kind – and we all know that you try to be fair, just, and loyal.'

Rita paused. Elizabeth listened, her heart thumping. Was Rita going to say that she must try again and perhaps be made a monitor next term, if she did well?

No – Rita was not going to say that. She smiled down at Elizabeth and went on: 'Well, Elizabeth, both William and I know you well by now, and we are quite sure that if we make you a monitor we shall not be disappointed in you. You will always treat other people better than you treat yourself – so we feel that it is quite safe to call you up to the monitors' table, and ask you to do your best for the school next term.'

With burning cheeks and shining eyes Elizabeth marched up to the Jury's table. She had never in her life felt so proud or so pleased. Oh, she didn't mind now not playing in the school concert – she didn't mind missing games and matches and gym! Her ill-luck had turned into a piece of marvellous *good* luck – she was actually a monitor – yes, really and truly one.

She took her place beside Joan, who squeezed her hand in delight. 'Jolly good!' said Joan. 'I *am* glad!'

And there we will leave Elizabeth, sitting at the monitors' table, dreaming of all the marvellous things she would do next term. A monitor! Could it really be true that the naughtiest girl in the school had become a monitor?

'I shall still do silly things, I expect, even now I'm a monitor,' thought Elizabeth, 'but never mind – I've got my chance! I'll show everybody something next term!'

And I expect she will!

If you can't wait
to read more about
The
Naughtiest Girl,
then turn over for
the beginning of her
next adventure...

The Naughtiest Girl is a monitor

1 Arabella comes to stay

It was in the middle of the Christmas holidays that Mother sprang a surprise on Elizabeth. Christmas was over, and Elizabeth had been to the pantomime and the circus, and to three parties.

Now she was beginning to look forward to going back to boarding-school again. It was dull being an only child, now that she had got used to living with so many girls and boys at Whyteleafe School. She missed their laughter and their chatter, the fun and games they had together.

'Mother, I love being at home – but I do miss Kathleen and Belinda and Nora and Harry and John and Richard,' she said. 'Joan has been over here to see me once or twice, but she's got a cousin staying with her now, and I don't expect I'll see her any more these hols.'

Then Mother gave Elizabeth a surprise.

'Well,' she said, 'I knew you would be lonely – so I have arranged for someone to come and keep you company for the last two weeks of these holidays, Elizabeth.'

'Mother! Who?' cried Elizabeth. 'Somebody I know?'

'No,' said Mother. 'It is a girl who is to go to Whyteleafe School next term – a girl called Arabella Buckley. I am sure you will like her.'

'Tell me about her,' said Elizabeth, still very surprised. 'Why didn't you tell me this before, Mother?'

'Well, it has been decided in a hurry,' said Mother. 'You know Mrs Peters, don't you? She has a sister who has to go to America, and she does not want to take Arabella with her. So she wanted to put the child into a boarding-school for a year, perhaps longer.'

'And she chose Whyteleafe School!' said Elizabeth. 'Well, it's the best school in the world, *I* think!'

'That's what I told Mrs Peters,' said Mother. 'And she told her sister – and Mrs Buckley at once went to see the headmistresses, Miss Belle and Miss Best . . .'

'The Beauty and the Beast,' said Elizabeth with a grin.

'And it was arranged that Arabella should go

to Whyteleafe this term,' went on Mother. 'As Mrs Buckley had to leave for America almost at once, I offered to have Arabella here – partly as company for you, and partly so that you might be able to tell her a little about Whyteleafe.'

'Mother, I do hope she's a nice sort of girl,' said Elizabeth. 'It will be fun sharing hols with someone I like, but awful if it's someone I don't like.'

'I have seen Arabella,' said Mother. 'She was a very pretty girl with most beautiful manners and she was dressed very nicely too.'

'Oh,' said Elizabeth, who was often untidily dressed, and was sometimes too impatient to have very good manners. 'Mother – I don't think I like the sound of her *very* much. Usually beautifully dressed girls aren't much good at games and things like that.'

'Well – you'll see,' said Mother. 'Anyway, she is coming tomorrow – so give her a good welcome and tell her as much about Whyteleafe as you can. I am sure she will love it.'

Elizabeth couldn't help looking forward to Arabella coming, even if she did sound rather goody-goody. She put flowers into the room her new friend was to have, and put beside the bed some of her own favourite books.

'It will be rather fun to tell someone all about Whyteleafe School,' she thought. 'I'm so proud of Whyteleafe. I think it's marvellous. And oh – I'm to be a *monitor* next term!'

Impatient, hot-tempered Elizabeth had actually been chosen to be a monitor for the coming term. It had been a great surprise to her, and she had been happier about that than about anything else in her life. She had often thought about it in the holidays, and planned how good and trustworthy and wise she would be next term.

'No quarrels with anyone – no bad tempers – no silly flare-ups!' said Elizabeth to herself. She knew her own faults very well. Indeed, all the children at Whyteleafe knew their faults, for it was part of the rule of the school that every child should be helped with his faults – and how could anyone be helped if his faults were not known?

The next day Elizabeth watched from the window for Arabella to come. In the afternoon a rather grand car drew up at the front door. The chauffeur got out and opened the car door – and out stepped someone who looked more like a little princess than a school-girl!

'Golly!' said Elizabeth to herself, and looked

down at her own school tunic of navy blue with its bright yellow badge. 'Golly! I shall never be able to live up to Arabella!'

Arabella was dressed in a beautiful blue coat with a white fur collar. She wore white fur gloves and a round white fur hat on her fair curls. Her eyes were very blue indeed and had dark lashes that curled up. She had a rather haughty look on her pink and white face as she stepped out of the car.

She looked at Elizabeth's house as if she didn't like it very much. The chauffeur rang the bell, and put a trunk and a bag down on the step.

Elizabeth had meant to rush down and give Arabella a hearty welcome. She had decided to call her 'Bella' because she thought Arabella rather a stupid name – 'like a doll's name,' thought Elizabeth. But somehow she didn't feel like calling her 'Bella' now.

'Arabella suits her better after all,' thought Elizabeth. 'She *is* rather like a doll with her golden curls and blue eyes, and lovely coat and hat. I don't think I like her. In fact – I think I feel a bit afraid of her!'

This was strange, because Elizabeth was rarely afraid of anything or anyone. But she had never before met anyone quite like Arabella Buckley.

'Although she's not much older than I am, she looks rather grown-up, and she walks like a grown-up – all proper – and I'm sure she talks like a grown-up too!' thought Elizabeth. 'Oh dear, I don't want to go down and talk to her.'

So she didn't go down. The maid opened the door – and then Mrs Allen, Elizabeth's mother, came hurrying forward to welcome the visitor.

She kissed Arabella, and asked her if she had had a tiring journey.

'Oh no, thank you,' said Arabella, in a clear, smooth voice. 'Our car is very comfortable, and I had plenty of sandwiches to eat halfway here. It is so kind of you to have me here, Mrs Allen. I hear you have a girl about my age.'

'Yes,' said Mrs Allen. 'She ought to be down here giving you a welcome. She said she would be. Elizabeth! Elizabeth, where are you? Arabella is here.'

So Elizabeth had to go down. She ran down the stairs in her usual manner, two at a time, landing with a bump at the bottom. She held out her hand to Arabella, who seemed a little surprised at her very sudden appearance.

'Do come down the stairs properly,' said Mrs Allen. It was a thing she said at least twelve times a day. Elizabeth never seemed able to remember to go anywhere quietly. Mrs Allen hoped that this nice, well-mannered Arabella would teach Elizabeth some of her own quietness and politeness.

'Hallo,' said Elizabeth, and Arabella held out a limp hand for her to shake.

'Good afternoon,' she said. 'How do you do?'

'Gracious!' thought Elizabeth, 'I feel as if she's Princess High-and-Mighty come to pay a call on one of her poor subjects. In a minute she'll be offering me a bowl of hot soup or a warm shawl.'

Still – it might be that Arabella was only feeling shy. Some people did go all stiff and proper when they felt shy. Elizabeth thought she had better give Arabella a chance before making up her mind about her.

'After all, I'm always making up my mind about people – and then having to unmake it because I am wrong,' thought the little girl. 'I've made an awful lot of mistakes about people at Whyteleafe School in the last two terms. I'll be careful now.'

So she smiled at Arabella and took her up to her room to wash and have a talk.

'I expect you didn't like saying goodbye to your mother, when she went off to America,' said Elizabeth in a pleasant voice. 'That was bad luck. But it's good luck for you to be going to Whyteleafe School. I can tell you that!'

'I shall be able to judge whether it is or not when I get there,' said Arabella. 'I hope to goodness there are decent children there.'

'Of course there are – and if they are horrid when they first come, we soon make them all right,' said Elizabeth. 'We had one or two boys who were awful – but now they are my best friends.'

'Boys! Did you say *boys*!' said Arabella in the greatest horror. 'I thought this was a girls' school I was going to. I hate boys!'

'It's a mixed school – boys and girls together,' said Elizabeth. 'It's fun. You won't hate boys after a bit. You soon get used to them.'

'If my mother had known there were boys at the school, I am sure she would not have sent me,' said Arabella in a tight, prim little voice. 'Rough, ill-mannered creatures – dirty and untidy, with shouting voices!'

'Oh, well – even the girls get dirty and untidy

sometimes,' said Elizabeth patiently, 'and as for shouting – you should just hear *me* when I'm watching a school match!'

'It sounds a terrible school to me,' said Arabella. 'I had hoped Mother would send me to Grey Towers, where two of my friends had gone – it's such a nice school. They all have their own pretty bedrooms – and wonderful food. In fact, the girls are treated like princesses.'

'Well – if you think you'll be treated like a princess at Whyteleafe, you'll jolly well find out you're wrong!' said Elizabeth sharply. 'You'll be treated as what you are – a little girl like me, with lots of things to learn! And if you put on any airs there, you'll soon be sorry, let me tell you that, Miss High-and-Mighty!'

'I think you are very rude, considering that I am a visitor, and have only just come,' said Arabella, looking down her nose in a way that made Elizabeth feel very angry. 'If that's the sort of manners they teach you at Whyteleafe, I am quite sure I shan't want to stay there more than a term.'

'I jolly well hope you don't stay a week!' said hot-tempered Elizabeth at once. She was sorry the moment after.

'Oh dear!' she said to herself. 'What a bad beginning! I really must be careful!'